Slightly Spooky Stories II

Patsy Collins

Contents

1. Facing The Music

The manager of the Solent Sound museum met me at the door. He still looked tired but there was no trace of panic in his face.

"Hello, Clive. How are things?" I asked.

"Good, thanks, Patricia."

Much to my relief he sounded as though he meant it. Clive seemed a different man from the one who'd made frantic calls about disappearing children, haunted organs and vengeful ex employees tormenting him from the grave. In fact he'd almost returned to how he was when I met him about six months previously.

Back then I'd just been appointed director of the museum group and had paid an unannounced visit to Solent Sound. I walked round first to get a feel for the place and found a group of unsupervised children messing about with an antique accordion.

Before I could say anything a volunteer rushed in and demanded they, "Stop that at once!" Her voice echoed around the tiled hall. She sent them outside, calling loudly for their teacher to get them under control.

The commotion brought Clive out of his office and when I saw his name badge I introduced myself and described the incident I'd witnessed.

"That woman!" Clive said.

"Perhaps she was a little sharp, but she had a point."

"I'm not so sure. We encourage people to come in here

and learn about musical instruments and yet insist they stay quiet and don't touch. It's not logical. These things were designed to be handled, to be played and enjoyed. How can we expect anyone, especially children, to appreciate them by staring at them through glass cabinets?"

I must have looked surprised for he continued, "I don't mean things like that accordion. That really should have been locked up safely and I'll take steps to ensure it is in future. Sturdier items could be tried out occasionally though, couldn't they? Triangles and xylophones and maybe we could buy in a few cheap second-hand instruments?"

"That's an excellent idea, Clive."

"Really?"

"Yes. Please go ahead. I can't promise much, but I'll allocate some funding."

"It'll have to wait until Muriel leaves. Hopefully that won't be much longer."

Muriel, I learned, was the volunteer I'd encountered earlier. Over the coming weeks I discovered she was also Clive's excuse for any delay, anything he failed to accomplish or which didn't go right.

It's true that Muriel seemed a little rigid and resistant to change. She was a retired schoolteacher so I guessed she found it hard to accept a position of absolutely no authority. Her idea of keeping things up to date was to retype information labels when they became too curled and faded to read.

Clive claimed she disliked people, youngsters in particular. Having people ask her questions was a source of irritation and she preferred to work in silence. Honestly, does that sound like someone who'd volunteer in a museum dedicated to musical instruments? She'd have to be mad.

"Try to include her more," I said when Clive complained about her for the third time in a week.

"I have. I asked her if she'd like to share her memories with children who visit the 'Swinging Sixties' display."

"Oh, good idea."

"She didn't think so. She said that even if she was old enough to be considered part of history, she wasn't prepared to be an exhibit to be poked and prodded and laughed at."

At the time I'd assumed he'd simply handled the situation without sufficient tact. Not long afterwards Muriel resigned. Although sad she'd left under a cloud of unhappiness and animosity, I was also slightly relieved. The personality clash between her and Clive had put everyone on edge.

For a while everything was great. Clive implemented his plan of providing instruments for people to try out on one day a week and it became extremely popular. Everyone from classes of school children to coachloads of nostalgic pensioners flocked in on 'noisy Wednesdays'. The café took more in that one day than in the rest of the week put together and the donations box saw plenty of use.

Muriel was almost forgotten until Clive received a letter saying she'd like to donate an item of her own; a very old and, judging by the photos, completely delightful steam organ. The kind with brightly coloured figures which lifted model trumpets to their painted lips or crashed cymbals and banged drums.

"It's a sign that she forgives you," I told him.

"I'm not so sure about that, but it'd be a brilliant thing to have here, especially if we could get it working."

With my encouragement he accepted her offer and I went

with him to see it. Shabby though it was, the instrument was glorious. If I was being fanciful, I'd have said it had life in it. The bandmaster held out his baton and the players clutched their instruments as though ready to play. The museum group couldn't really afford to have it restored, but we got a bit of local sponsorship, sold a few items and somehow scraped together enough to send the organ off for restoration.

Originally it would have been powered by a steam engine. There wasn't one with it and in any case it wouldn't have been practical or safe to run one inside, but the restorer informed us that it could be adapted to run off electricity without damage to any original features.

"All it needs is a different sized drive belt and it'll soon be thumping out a tune."

"Muriel won't like that," Clive said. He looked quite worried.

As if to prove him right, Muriel died the very Monday the refurbished organ was brought into the museum. It seemed a shame she wouldn't get to see it in all its glory.

Even still and silent the organ was magnificent. The metalwork gleamed and the figures of the band members each wore a bright new coat of paint. Each of them was different and although exaggerated caricatures, somehow quite realistic. I was sure they'd been modelled on real people. You can imagine how eager we were to see the figures move and hear the music pour out.

We'd have given it a test run, but after it had been set up in pride of place in the main hall it was discovered that the power lead wouldn't quite reach the socket.

"Soon sort that out, don't worry," the restorer said, but he didn't return that day or the next and wouldn't answer his telephone.

On the next 'noisy Wednesday' a grand unveiling was planned, with local dignitaries and press invited along with all the nearby primary children. The post arrived at the same time as the first guests. The only item was a letter from Muriel, sent via her solicitor. She wrote that she'd heard what had been done with her organ and that she'd made a big mistake in donating it. She'd thought it would be safe here and would have had it melted down rather than risk it being played. She insisted it remain silent and that a rope should be put up around it so no one could touch it.

"Can she do that?" Clive asked. "She gave it to the museum and I have a receipt to prove it."

"I don't know, Clive. I don't think we should risk playing it until we've had our legal team look into the matter."

The fact that Muriel had waited until after we'd had it refurbished seemed like spite to me. Although sure he'd been exaggerating, I was starting to think there was truth behind Clive's complaints about Muriel. Because of that I had a rope put up and ordered that it not be touched until I'd consulted our lawyers.

I was disappointed to leave without hearing a tune and seeing the little figures dance and play, but thought I wouldn't have long to wait before it could be switched on.

As it turned out it was a blessing we didn't get it working in front of the assembled crowd. That night, as Clive prepared to lock up, he noticed the cable by then reached to the power socket. As a safety precaution he unplugged it and saw the casing was cracked and damp.

"If I'd switched it on I'd probably have got a shock and ended up joining Muriel!"

He rang the restorer for an explanation, but he still wasn't answering his phone. Clive had the plug replaced and the wiring double checked, so the organ was ready to play the moment he got the go ahead.

"Have you noticed anything about the bandmaster?" Clive asked.

I peered closely at the figure. "Oh, it's a woman! That's unusual I should think."

"I've done some research and yes, it's very unusual. Does she remind you of anyone?"

"Yes… Muriel. Perhaps that's why she bought it?" I suggested. "It's a curious thing for her to have owned."

"There's something very odd about it altogether," he said.

Clive rang me in a panic the following week. "A child climbed up on the organ and now he's gone. Muriel's taken him, I know she has!"

I couldn't calm him down by phone, so went over.

"I'll prove it," he said and took me to the organ. "Just there, look!"

The figure he indicated did indeed look like a schoolboy, but then so did some of the others. The idea that a dead woman was so annoyed by a child climbing on the organ that she'd transform him into a part of it was, of course, ridiculous.

Oddly the picture in the paper of the missing boy really did look rather like the figure on the organ. Apparently he was a troubled lad who frequently broke the rules and had run away more than once. All the staff and some visitors were questioned by the police and the resulting publicity meant the museum was much quieter than usual for a time afterwards.

"That's what she wanted. That's why she took him," Clive said.

That had me worried, but he seemed to pull himself together and to my shame I was more concerned about the museum's reputation than his state of mind.

Other than learning that the restorer never sent an invoice and couldn't be contacted, I didn't hear anything about the organ for a couple of weeks. The lawyers hadn't replied to my question about the legalities of playing it against the previous owners wishes and oddly Clive didn't ask about the situation either. I was busy with other things so didn't give it much thought. Then Clive summoned me to point out that one of the figures bore a resemblance to a man who'd been sleeping rough in the area.

"He used to come in on cold days," Clive told me. "I let him stay until I locked up and if there were sandwiches or anything left over in the café I gave them to him. Muriel wouldn't have wanted someone like that anywhere near the place, but he seemed like a nice person underneath and he loved music. I… You remember how cold it was last week?"

I nodded. The papers had been full of alarmist stories that the 'big freeze' would last for weeks despite the fact everything had thawed out again before the early editions were printed.

"I saw him curled up behind a display as I did my final check, but pretended I hadn't and locked him in. I know I shouldn't have let him stay, but …"

I nodded again. Of course he shouldn't have done it, but I'm not sure I could have chucked out someone I knew had nowhere to go on a night like that.

"He wasn't here in the morning and no one has seen him since."

"Then he didn't stay the night. Either you only thought you saw him there, or he slipped out as you finished your checks. You said yourself he often stayed until the last minute. He probably got into a shelter somewhere and they're helping him, that's why he hasn't been back."

Clive grew ever more fanciful. Whenever there was an appeal to locate a missing person he'd study the organ to see if their face matched a figure on the organ. On Wednesdays he'd keep racing to the organ to check the notes he could hear weren't coming from it. When the caretaker died from a heart attack he said it was because he'd touched the organ as he swept up.

The final straw was when he rang up screaming, "I'm next! I saw the drummer. She's going to get me next."

Worried he was close to a breakdown, I suggested he seek help and take a few days off work.

"I can't. If I'm not there someone might switch on the organ. I have to make sure they don't."

"I have some good news about that actually. Our lawyers have looked into it and there's no reason we have to take any notice of Muriel's final request. She made absolutely no mention of any terms or conditions when she donated it and she could easily have done so then. They confirm it legally belongs to the museum trust and we can play it if we wish."

"I don't think we should," Clive said. "It wouldn't be right. Muriel wasn't threatening us in the letter, she was warning us."

"Of course we should. That was the… Hang on, have you not had a day off since it arrived?"

He hadn't. He'd worked six days a week, including late openings on Wednesdays and Saturdays for months. No wonder he was so stressed.

"Clive, you are taking the rest of this week and next Monday and Tuesday off work. On Wednesday I'll come in and we'll play the organ."

As we'd arranged, I drove over to the Solent Sound museum the following week, shortly before opening time. Clive met me at the door. He still looked a bit tired, but nowhere near as jumpy as he'd been in the previous few weeks. I felt bad that I'd not been a bit more supportive.

"So, we'll go and get that organ started, shall we?" I suggested.

"It was your idea to get it restored, so you should have the honour." Clive swept open the gallery door for me.

I saw someone had already removed the rope barrier and 'keep off' notices. They'd even put the plug into its socket.

"I've got it all ready for you," Clive said.

"So you're over your fear of it now?"

"Like you said, I was tired and let my imagination get the better of me. Can you believe I thought that drummer there looked like me?"

I looked from Clive's bearded face to that of the woman with drumsticks in her hand. Of course she looked nothing like him. In fact she looked much more like me. Her eyes and hair were the same colour as mine. She even had a tiny freckle in just the same place as I do. How odd that I'd never noticed that or the puzzled frown on her face.

Clive was right, there definitely was something odd about that organ I thought, as I reached out to switch it on.

2. Enchanting

"Absolutely enchanting. You simply must have it," Mademoiselle gushed as Daphne emerged from the changing room. Daphne, remembering the price tag, was not surprised at her enthusiasm. She stood before the mirror and smiled.

"Mademoiselle's right; you do look good," Marie whispered. The dress was wonderful, suiting her perfectly. Her skin looked clearer, brighter; as if her body lotion was for once living up to its advertising. Her long hair looked sleek instead of just straight. The colour rich and deep not just brown.

"It's an investment," Marie advised.

Daphne looked Mademoiselle straight in the eye and explained that although the dress was superb it cost more than she could afford. She smiled persuasively and bought the dress at a generous discount. It really did seem to cast a spell.

Daphne was looking forward to the school reunion. What a change from the one held five years ago. She hadn't gone. The memories of the teasing she'd received there as a pupil were enough to put her off. That combined with her lack of both employment and a love life meant she just hadn't been able to face it.

After the event she'd been sent some photographs of people doing daft things. The classroom heart throb, losing his hair and gaining a paunch, was caught with a beer in one hand and the ample bottom of an ex-classmate in the other. 'Don't tell his wife!!!' the caption read. Another showed Marie, the only girl who'd been taunted more than Daphne. Marie had gained weight steadily all through school and well beyond. 'Don't tell Weight Watchers!!!' captioned a picture showing Marie shovelling in chocolate gateaux. Daphne remembered Marie as the butt of every joke. Marie had desperately wanted her friendship. Daphne, to her shame, had never spoken against the cruel treatment of Marie.

Daphne located her old address book. She'd never bothered phoning Marie, but had taken her number. She wasn't surprised to find that Marie still lived at home.

"I missed the reunion, how was it?" Daphne asked.

"About like you would expect."

"You mean everyone claimed to have perfect lives themselves, bitched about everyone else and you in particular?"

"Well…"

"Thought so. Look, I know I was maybe a bit spiteful at school, I've changed. What about you, haven't you ever wanted to stop being the victim?"

Marie agreed to meet Daphne, who explained her ideas. "Everyone enjoys laughing at other people's silly actions. For the right person that reunion could have been fun, filled with opportunities."

Not just there, works parties, wedding receptions, birthdays, graduations, all had potential. Suitable occasions happened every day. All that was required was an ability to manipulate. A little tact and charm would enable her to turn other people's dire behaviour to her own advantage.

Everyone, given the right provocation could be tempted to behave out of character. There were plenty of fools out there willing to get themselves into embarrassing situations and pay for the privilege.

"Do you want to help me? I could do it alone, but it would be easier and more fun if we did it together."

At first Marie was reluctant, but she looked at Daphne's eager face and agreed. "I've nothing to lose have I?"

They began immediately, training separately, and working together on their scheme. Marie provided the funds. Daphne felt no guilt over this, it was the reason she'd invited Marie to join her. Soon they'd both be making a profit. On Tuesdays Marie attended sessions with a local slimming group. Daphne told her constantly that she could lose the weight, both Marie and the scales began to believe her.

Daphne took photography evening classes. Ability in that area would be very useful in their new venture. They'd need plenty of evidence to keep the money rolling in. They mixed with lots of people, becoming popular and in demand at all the most lucrative venues.

Daphne's new skills were soon in use on a regular basis. They'd achieved success often, but always with strangers. The second school reunion was to be the first occasion they would work amongst those they knew. They could make people who'd been cruel, suffer. Daphne knew she could humiliate them. She was practised at spotting people's weaknesses and exploiting them.

"Don't go too far," Marie pleaded.

"You're too kind for your own good. There are more than a few people who deserve to be on the receiving end of a joke for once, and we have our livings to earn."

"I know, and I'm not against seeing the worst of them squirm a little, but I don't want people to be as hurt as I was."

Daphne nodded, but didn't reply. She brushed her hair until it shone. She applied dramatic makeup to her eyes, her best feature. She slipped into the dress, knowing people would not be able to resist looking at her. Marie dressed far more conservatively, nobody one would be looking in her direction.

The reunion was fun. A girl who was now a nightclub singer belted out a few cheerful numbers. One man did stand up as a hobby. They all laughed until it hurt and everyone voted that he go professional. Daphne and Marie were working too, confident they could pick up quite a bit of business here. They were pleased so many of those they'd studied with seemed to be doing well. They would be able to pay.

Daphne danced with the men, openly flirting. As they looked deep into her eyes she felt confident and powerful. They were eager to do whatever she wanted. She chatted to the girls too. Several of them confided in her. She made a point of being easy to talk to. People told her things they were surprised they'd let slip when later reminded. There was a great deal of laughter and more than one sheepish look when people realised they'd done things for the benefit of Marie's camera they would not normally have done. Others still were in blissful ignorance of what would develop.

Well, they would find out when they got the photographs. Daphne and Marie volunteered to get them printed and distributed. A smile lit Marie's face as she wrote the address of a girl who had once made too many cruel remarks about her greedy eating habits. The girl was pictured cramming chocolate éclairs in her mouth, exactly as if she believed that was the only food she had eaten all week.

The lad who'd been the worst bully was shown dancing on a table in an improvised pink tutu. His former accomplice appeared to be terrified of the paper napkin he was being offered. One snobby girl was seen to be trying to hide her fully clothed body with a flower arrangement as if she imagined she was naked.

The comic had never taunted either of them. His photo showed laughing friends applauding wildly. The girls enclosed a note about agency services for performers. He truly was good enough to become professional.

Another photograph showed the one time school heart throb on his knees, a rose between his teeth as he serenaded Marie.

The girls laughed together as they recalled the party.

"Thanks, Daphne. That was far more fun than the last reunion, and I'm sure it will be really good for business."

"Good job I've got you to handle all the bookings that are going to flood in. And to talk me out of blackmail and into the safer, kinder world of the entertainment business."

At last all the envelopes were addressed and sealed. Each contained a photograph and a business card, neatly embossed with, 'Daphne Devine – Hypnotist.'

3. Lost And Found

Joshua Clarke lifted the needle on the gramophone and stepped into the hall to answer the telephone.

"I'm sorry but we've lost Phyllis." Those words told him his bride to be was gone from his life. She wasn't lost like a dropped bus ticket to be picked up again if he retraced his steps. She was gone forever and nothing could bring her back. The life they'd planned together was lost. Their future was lost. Joshua was lost.

He had to continue to live. He couldn't put their families through more grief. So he breathed and ate and walked and talked. He couldn't live in the flat they'd leased, ready for the life they'd never share. It was decorated in the pretty colours and patterns she'd chosen. A few of their wedding gifts had already been delivered.

Joshua couldn't continue in the job he'd thought would provide for his wife and the children they'd hoped to have. He continued to live with his family. No, not lived; existed.

It was his brother who'd seen the advert. "They want someone in the lost and found office, Joshua. Might suit you?"

He knew about loss. "You think I might find happiness there?" It didn't seem likely.

"Worth a try maybe. Anyway you wouldn't be any less happy there earning your keep than you would be stopping home all day."

That had been the push he'd needed. He didn't want to be a financial burden on this family any more than he wanted to be an emotional one. Joshua applied for the job and got it. That news didn't cheer him exactly but it lifted the gloom a little.

The first thing handed in, after he'd learnt the ropes and been left on his own, was a radio. He logged it in just as he'd been shown, not expecting it to stay long.

Three days later his mum sat beside him on the sofa and squeezed his hand. She did that when he'd sat with tears streaming down his face thinking of Phyllis. This time though her worried frown was replaced by a hopeful smile.

"How's your job going, love?"

"Good, Mam. Funny the things people leave behind. There's this lovely little radio. Must have cost a bit but no one's claimed it. Weird thing is the initials painted on it are the same as mine."

"That's what you were thinking about?"

"Yes, oh." It was him she was still worried about. "Yes, Mam. I was thinking about work."

She hugged him. "I'm so pleased you took the job."

"Yes, me too. The money will help you and …"

"Not because of the money. Make us a brew, shall I?"

Joshua nodded. That radio. Maybe it didn't work, that's why it hadn't been claimed. He'd test it at work the following day.

It worked fine. The moment he turned the dial a cheerful song, by some new chap called Presley, filled his small office. He found himself singing along as he worked. The days whizzed by with a constant stream of dropped items. Pens, handkerchiefs, books of various kinds, bags and boxes, walking sticks, umbrellas and items of clothing were everyday occurrences. It was good to reunite them with their owners, but he found dealing with the more unusual items the most satisfying. For one thing it was interesting to see what kind of person could mislay their false teeth or glass eye. The less common items also seemed to hold the most value to those who reclaimed them. A very attractive woman was delighted to get back the diary which she used to manage what was obviously a busy social life. A small boy squealed with delight at the sight of his toy train and a little girl's tears disappeared when Joshua produced her dropped teddy bear.

A wallet of cash was handed in one day. Joshua found identification and bank details inside, but decided to hold on to it for the day. The owner would probably try his office before contacting her bank. A distressed, but still pretty, lady came in just as he was about to lock up.

"I wonder if anyone has handed in a wallet?"

"Could you describe it and give me your name?"

She was extremely grateful to discover all the money was still there.

"What a relief! Aren't you ever tempted to keep things?"

"No, I know the pain of losing something that you thought would be yours forever."

"Oh. Well, the money isn't for anything permanent but I do think it's important. We provide short holidays for sick and disabled children. They have a nice time and their families get a much needed break." She extracted a note. "I'd like to give you a reward for your honesty."

"Thank you, but you keep it for the kids."

A few days later she returned with a cake for him. He

accepted that and chatted to her for a while. She visited several times and dropped a few hints about her lack of a boyfriend and liking for the cinema. Joshua discussed films with her but didn't invite her to watch one. She was pretty and pleasant… but not Phyllis.

Joshua did find happiness of a kind. He was good at his job and considered it worthwhile. He kept meticulous records but rarely needed them due to his wonderful memory. He didn't forget Phyllis. He didn't want to. Maybe it was just cowardice about facing that pain again. Joshua guessed he'd remain single.

After a few years Joshua began making plans for his future. He applied for and got another job, one that gave him the chance of a career. His old boss called him back as he left the lost property office.

"Aren't you going to take your radio?"

Joshua was about to protest it wasn't his, but stopped himself. It did feel like his somehow, and it was unlikely it would be claimed now. He took it and noted in the records that he'd done so.

"If the true owner ever claims it I'll return it."

When he retired from his career Joshua was still single. He often visited his brother's family, but without work to fill his days began to feel lonely and bored. He didn't realise what he was doing until he found himself outside the lost property office. He smiled; it was an appropriate place to visit as he did indeed feel lost.

"Can I help you?" a pregnant young woman asked.

"Sorry, I just came to look. I used to work here, many years ago."

"Come on in and have a look if you like. I expect it's

changed a lot?"

It had in some ways. Joshua' ledgers were replaced by computers and the lost items were now mostly phones and iPods. People seemed less likely to go searching for lost items, preferring instead to buy new, so the office only opened part time, but for all the differences it was basically the same.

"Don't fancy coming back do you?" the young woman asked. "I'm leaving soon." She patted her baby bump. "The person who was going to stand in for me changed their mind."

Joshua sat in with Wendy for a few days to learn how to use the computer system. By the time he'd got the hang of it his previous employers had been contacted for a reference and Joshua was offered the job, two short days a week.

He took the radio with him. Joshua really enjoyed the job. He saw a huge range of mobile phones whose owners were delighted to get them back. Mostly though the people who had time to come and enquire about lost items were lonely and wanted a chat as much as they wanted to reclaim a dropped glove or lost comb. When Wendy came in with her baby, he was pleased to see them both looking well and happy, but saddened that she'd soon return to work and he'd no longer be needed.

On his last day the door was pushed open by a young man. Despite the warm spring weather a cold draft seemed to come in with him.

"I think you know why I'm here, Joshua," the stranger said in a gentle voice.

He shook his head as though to dislodge the thought forming there.

"I've come for my radio," the man said.

Despite the fact the man wasn't old enough to have been born at the time the radio was handed in he told Joshua exactly where and when the radio was lost and described it accurately, even the painted initials. He couldn't have found it out from the ledgers Joshua had written as they'd all been destroyed years ago. Playing for time Joshua did a search of the computer records but of course found nothing. He knew though that he'd have to hand it over.

"Why now? Why are you taking it from me now?"

"You don't need it now. I'm just claiming what I've lost and now it's time for you to do the same."

The music from the radio changed to singing more beautiful than Joshua had ever heard. The man gestured to the doorway. Through it streamed a beautiful light. As his eyes adjusted Joshua made out the shape of a girl standing just beyond the threshold.

It was Phyllis. They'd found each other again.

4. Cannibal's Hymn

Louise attempted to ignore the hungry people who surrounded her. She tried not to watch them rub their hands and lick their lips. She wasn't able to avoid hearing them mutter horribly. She was too upset to listen to the words and tried to be grateful that at least the noise blocked out the sounds of their rumbling stomachs. It sounded as though they were praying or, even more terribly, saying grace before dinner.

Feeling like a juicy burger, sizzling on a barbecue grill, Louise sucked in her stomach, hunched her shoulders and tried to look as small and unappealing as possible. She'd been really skinny when she was younger. People said she had no meat on her – how she wished she still matched up to that description. It was of no comfort to remember that only days before she'd been wishing boys would think she was tasty. Sweat dripped down from her face and glistened on her arms and legs. It reminded her of basting a succulent joint with meat juices. Despite the tropically humid atmosphere, Louise shivered.

Thinking about roast dinners and flame grilled snacks wasn't helping at all. It wasn't just the heat from the glowing coals that was making her sweat; it was fear. She was the only stranger, trapped in here with villagers who didn't like outsiders, but did want a meal. The conversations of those around her didn't help improve her mood.

"I like a nice crisp green salad, with caesar dressing, to go with mine," said a woman who's bright red suit was under considerable strain.

"Really?" her friend asked.

Louise could understand her scepticism; the woman in red didn't look as though she ate much salad. Louise simply wouldn't allow herself to consider what she did eat. Neither would she acknowledge her own hunger. That would only make her more acutely aware of how the others felt.

"I'd rather have a jacket potato," red woman's friend said.

"What about some ripe tomatoes, drizzled with balsamic vinegar?" Red asked.

Louise swallowed the lump that formed in her throat and then wished she hadn't. It was better not to think about anything to do with swallowing.

Why on earth had she let Cindy talk her into coming here? Cindy, of course, wasn't trapped. Louise could only hope her friend really had gone for help and that the help would arrive in time.

The trip had started well enough with a scenic drive through the countryside and the pair of them singing along to CDs. Even when her muscles were being pummelled and her skin rubbed with herb infused oils, Louise had felt relaxed. Of course, that's before she'd realised the truth about this place. Now that pleasantly calm feeling had vanished and Louise realised there was little difference between a soothing massage and being tenderised and marinated. In fact, no difference at all.

Perhaps she should try to think of something else? If she could just stay calm until she was rescued, then maybe she wouldn't be roasted and… She refused to consider what would happen if Cindy didn't reach the appropriate authorities in time.

What was that song they'd listened to on the way here? Was it something about being down by the sea? She was sure it was. Thinking about cool water was a good idea. If she were to close her eyes and imagine she was by the beach instead of trapped in this hot steamy hell hole with a bunch of savages then she could get through this. She'd dream of a cool stream and …that was it! She remembered a line from the song, about dreaming by a river. Moonlight came into it somewhere too and there was definitely mention of a happy ending.

That was more like it, Louise thought. Don't think about the heat, or the hard wooden plank that's supporting you, or that you can barely move, let alone walk away. Who was the song by? She tried to remember. It had been playing on the radio when Cindy had first suggested the two of them go away together for the weekend. Louise had just split up with her boyfriend and Cindy was trying to cheer her up. As she'd talked about the idea, she'd been searching the internet on her phone.

"It'd be good for you to be a bit adventurous and try something new. I can get a really cheap last minute deal."

It had seemed like a bargain. Now she knew why the cost was so low. This place was so backward it was as though cavemen… Aha! Nick Cave, that's who'd sung the song! She could remember some more words too. Banging drums and gongs, something like that. Then when she remembered the part about those who dine with cannibals getting eaten, it was Louise who was banging on the door, trying once again to raise the alarm.

"No!" she screamed. "Let me free!"

"Calm down, love," said the lady next to her. "I'm sure it will be all right."

The lady didn't look sure, but Louise appreciated the words of comfort and smiled at her. She'd almost forgotten that although the only outsider, she wasn't the only person who was trapped.

"Thanks," she whispered.

"Your friend went for help, didn't she?"

"Yes. Cindy won't let us down. Somehow she'll get us out of here."

Louise realised the others had heard her words.

"Are you sure about that?" Red asked.

"Yes!" Louise assured them.

She was right. A few minutes later the door was forced open and everyone was able to leave.

"Sorry we got so annoyed with you," one of the villagers said. "It's your first visit to this spa, so you weren't to know the sauna door sticks if you don't close it just right."

5. A Lucky Find

"What's up, Sally?" Linda said as she walked into her sister's office.

"I've lost my lucky locket. Someone's probably found it and decided to keep it."

"Like you did?" Linda asked.

"That was different! I was meant to find it. Destiny or something, you know?"

Linda looked sceptical. "I think it's a good thing you've lost it. You've been relying on that locket to make things work out for you instead of solving your own problems or listening to the concerns of your family."

"Is this going to be another lecture about smoking?"

"No; I'm not going to waste my breath, nor with suggesting you treat people better. You're probably blaming your assistant for stealing the locket. And you're probably even grumpier than usual at home and expecting Bill to pander to you while you completely ignore how he feels. Sometimes I wonder why he puts up with you."

"What are you; his guardian angel or something? How about showing some support for your sister for a change?"

"Sally, I've always been supportive, you just can't see it because I don't always say what you want to hear. I don't see why I'm getting it in the neck because you've lost something that was never yours to start with."

"I'm going to have bad luck."

Linda squeezed her hand. "Come on, that's daft. Even if the locket really was lucky, you won't have bad luck without it, just the normal luck the rest of us get."

"I suppose."

"Why don't you wear that lovely gold locket Bill bought you for your anniversary? Maybe that will be lucky too?"

When she did and saw how pleased he was, Sally wished she'd worn it earlier and been more appreciative when he'd given it to her. She'd said the pattern had worn off the one she'd found because she'd needed to polish it regularly in order to prevent the tarnishing staining her neck green. He'd probably thought that was a hint she'd like a new one. Even if he didn't always get it right, he did try.

Sally's annoying cough seemed to have worsened since the day she lost the lucky locket. She knew Bill worried about her smoking; perhaps she should see the doctor, just to set his mind at rest?

It wasn't until the doctor reminded her yet again of the dangers of heavy smoking, and said only luck had so far saved her from a serious smoking related illness, Sally realised how much trouble she was in. With no lucky locket to help her, smoking was an unacceptable risk.

Bill was delighted she intended to stop. He went with her to the Saturday clinic despite it meaning he'd miss the cricket on TV.

"I recorded the game for you," she said when they arrived home. "You switch it on and I'll bring you a drink."

"I love you," Bill said, hugging her.

"I know. I love you, too." She couldn't remember the last time she'd said that.

She made them both a coffee and took Bill his. "Where's

the ashtray?"

"I've thrown them and your lighters and a couple of packs of cigarettes in the bin."

"What?" Sally shrieked.

"You won't be needing them again. You've got the patches and everything."

"Patches! Do you know how difficult it is not to smoke? You threw them out when I was getting ready to go to the clinic, didn't you?"

"I thought it would be easier if you didn't see them when you came back."

"You thought! You thought wrong."

"Calm down, love. How about coming to golf with me on Sunday? At the clinic, they said it's good to break your routine to help break the habit and getting some fresh air in your lungs might do you good."

"Don't you dare patronise me!" Sally stormed upstairs and rang Linda.

Her sister, as usual, took Bill's side. "He was trying to help. The cravings are making you irritable, try not to take it out on him."

Sally didn't speak to either of them for the rest of the weekend. A couple of restless nights didn't help Sally's mood, but what really angered her was arriving at work to find her lighter, ashtray and almost full pack of cigarettes missing.

"Your husband called and said you'd given up and asked me to get rid of anything that might tempt you," her assistant, Julie, said.

"I'm your boss, not him and the next thing to be got rid of might be you if you steal things from me."

"I haven't stolen anything. All your disgusting smoking stuff is in a bag under your desk. While we're on the subject, I never touched your locket and didn't appreciate your hints that I may have."

They worked without speaking until Julie offered to make a cup of tea. Sally grudgingly accepted and by the end of the day, things were almost back to normal. Sally didn't smoke. She wouldn't give Julie the satisfaction of weakening in front of her.

Sally remembered all the times she'd nagged Bill about spending time and money on his golf instead of her and he'd pointed out how much she spent on cigarettes and that he'd love her to come to golf with him. Maybe it was only luck Bill hadn't yet got fed up with her nagging and gone off with someone who shared his interests. Her younger, ladies golf champion sister, for example.

"Bill, would you like me to come to golf next Sunday?" she asked when she got in.

"Very much."

Bill's friends at the golf club were very welcoming. Linda was pleased to see her too. Sally's foolish thoughts of jealousy disappeared, even before Sally noticed the way Linda looked at the rather attractive young man who was acting as her caddy.

At work on Monday, she asked her assistant if the quarterly report was ready.

"No, I'm really sorry," Julie said.

Sally started to snap about inefficiency and stomp off for a cigarette when she realised being unable to do the latter might be contributing to her desire to do the former.

"Are you nearly finished? I'll need it this afternoon," she

asked quietly.

"Almost; I'll definitely have it ready for you to read through before the meeting starts."

"That's OK, then. Sorry I snapped. It's probably because I'm not smoking and I'm used to these reports being on my desk first thing in the morning."

"They will be in future. My daughter is in a school play and I've been making her costume and helping her learn her lines this weekend so I was short of time. I'll plan ahead better in future."

"I'll leave you to it, then," Sally said.

It was time she wrote Julie's staff report. Actually, it was past time and Julie had already given three tactful reminders. Sally would write it now and this time she'd make it as accurate as Julie's work. It wasn't loyalty that kept Julie working for her – it was the lacklustre reports that ruined Julie's promotion chances. Maybe if Sally were nicer she could inspire the kind of loyalty that would enable her to keep staff. She put the kettle on. She had to guess how Julie liked it, but the pack of sweeteners by the kettle was a clue.

"Thank you," Julie whispered.

"Every time I feel like going out for a smoke, I'll make tea instead."

"There's no need ..."

"No and there's no need for you to take work home. Just tell me if I've not given you time to do something."

Now, where was the woman's personnel file? She'd seen it a few days ago.

Sally rummaged through a rarely used draw and found the file – and her missing locket. She opened the locket and looked at the picture of her and Bill taken the day he asked her to marry him. She undid the chain from her new locket and laid it open alongside the old one. Sally met Bill shortly after she'd found the first locket. She'd been walking across the park and remembering her previous fall in the mud and resulting lucky find, she'd kept her attention firmly on where she was putting her feet. That's why she'd been oblivious of the group of lads playing frisbee.

Bill had been very apologetic when his throw struck her shoulder. It hadn't really hurt, but she'd accepted his offer to buy her a hot drink for the shock. Since then, so many things had gone right for her; wonderful wedding, good job Bill had helped her study for, lovely home they'd made together.

Sally removed the older photograph and placed it in the locket from Bill.

"Julie, perhaps your daughter would like this?" she said, handing her the old locket. "It'll help her remember her lines."

"But that's your lucky locket! You were so upset when you lost it."

"I was, but that's before I realised it had already brought me more luck than I deserve and all I'll ever need."

6. Seeing The Truth

Lydia Beckley read her horoscope. 'A romantic concern has been troubling you recently. There's no need for secrecy. Put aside you usual Libran tact for now is the time to act.' Lydia folded the paper thoughtfully. The horoscope was wrong, of course. She was in a delicate position and would need all her tact in the next few weeks. Any hint of scandal or trouble regarding Lydia or her department could ruin her promotion prospects. She made her way down the corridor toward Peter Edgar's classroom.

The horoscope had got one thing right, Lydia was troubled by a romantic concern. She now knew where Peter's romantic interest lay but had completely overreacted when she discovered the truth and caused trouble. Since then, she'd been trying to put things right. She'd dropped subtle hints, but to no avail. Maybe it was time to tackle him directly. She took a deep breath, fastened a smile to her face and walked in.

Peter was at his desk, but he wasn't alone. Sharon from 5b had drawn up a chair and was sitting so close, her long fair locks brushed against his short dark hair as they bent their heads over a sheet of paper. Whatever was written there obviously amused them for Peter gave a wry smile and Sharon was giggling. Lydia cleared her throat – loudly.

Both of them looked up. Both blushed.

"Well, I think that's everything, Sharon," he mumbled.

"Yes, sir," she said as she grabbed the paper and slunk

away.

"Peter, I think we should talk."

"Er, yes."

He looked relieved. As they looked at each other, Lydia wished she'd thought through what she wanted to say. Anything would be better than nothing.

"Sharon is a bright kid," she said.

"Yes. I'm, er, helping her with a, um, special project."

"Right."

"For the school fête. You'll be going, won't you?"

"Of course. All the teaching staff and many of the parents will be there, Peter."

"I understand. Best behaviour, nothing that could cause any rumours."

Lydia wasn't at all sure he had understood, but as the bell rang for the next lesson she had to go.

She couldn't be sure, but it seemed to her Peter avoided her after that. He still wished her a good morning and joined in with staffroom chatter, but whenever it seemed she might get a word alone with him, he either said he had work to do, or simply melted away.

Lydia took extra care with her appearance for the school fête. It seemed Peter had too. His dark, thick hair was brushed to glossy perfection, he was freshly shaved and his crisp shirt and dark trousers neatly ironed. He gave her his trademark cheeky grin. No wonder half the girls had a crush on him.

"Peter, can I have a word when you're free?" she asked at the earliest opportunity.

"Yes. Tell you what, you go have your fortune told and I'll

meet you afterwards."

"Sharon knows what's in store for me, does she?"

"Well," he shrugged and turned away, but not before she'd seen the return of his guilty blush.

Lydia entered the dimly lit tent and crossed the girl's palm with silver. She had to admit the costume was really good, as was Sharon's act. Even though Lydia knew perfectly well who sat, dealing cards, across the small table from her it was hard to recognise the heavily made up Sharon. Amazing what fake tan, hair dye and a whole heap of accessories can do. Even her voice and manner were different as she gave Lydia some vague information about her life. It was all reasonably accurate, but so generic it didn't seem as though Sharon had done her homework. A few questions to other staff members would have yielded more specific revelations.

After a pause for dramatic effect the 'gypsy' said, "You've been troubled by matters of love."

"Yes."

"And by rumours and gossip."

"No." She was sure there was no gossip and she was simply reacting to her own observations.

"Not yet, but you fear them."

That was true. She did worry what people might say and how Peter's employers might react to those rumours.

"There's nothing for you to fear."

Easy for her to say. What did a fifteen-year-old really know of love and career prospects? Lydia wished the girl weren't holding her hand and staring into her eyes as she spoke. She frowned, she was sure Sharon's eyes were brown, not vivid blue. Was she wearing contacts?

"You love a water carrier."

Lydia nodded. Peter's star sign was Aquarius.

"You want to know what to do?"

"Not really, I've already decided to say something."

She'd expected the girl to react strongly to that. Instead she just looked thoughtful. "Actions speak louder than words."

"That's true."

Lydia left the tent in search of Peter. She found him talking to a group of school governors.

She kissed his cheek and put her arm through his.

"Excuse us," he mumbled before steering her away. "What are you doing, Lydia?"

"You still like me, I know you do."

"Yes, but you turned me down. Was it really just because of your application to be deputy head?"

"Yes, but I've changed my mind. Sure, some people will think I've rushed into this relationship too quickly after my divorce, but really it's no concern of theirs and anyway, it might not affect my job prospects."

"So, you'll come out with me?"

"Yes." Remembering the words she'd just heard, about actions speaking louder than words, Lydia kissed him. Properly this time.

They returned to the group of governors. A few smiled, one winked, but no one looked horrified. Sharon was right, she had nothing to fear.

"Excuse me, Miss Beckley?" The gypsy whispered to her and gestured for her to follow.

"What's wrong, Sharon?" Lydia asked.

"That's just it. I'm not Sharon. I'm her older sister. Sharon was really ill this morning and asked me to fill in. I reckon I've got a gift for this so I was happy to give it a go. Trouble is I just got a text off her. She wrote down what she was going to say and wanted me to read it to you, but I got the message too late. She's really worried we've messed things up."

"Tell her Mr Edgar will give her an A for her performance today. I think she'll understand."

"I'm not sure I do."

"You keep looking into people's palms and you'll find you do."

7. Before The Paint Dries

"We've had some lovely comments about your work, Claire," Mrs Dalgetty said as she greeted them at the entrance to the art exhibition.

"Oh good. Everything is going OK, I hope?" Claire asked. She felt Harvey give her hand a reassuring squeeze.

"Very well. We've been busy all day and made some sales already."

That wasn't quite what Claire had meant, but surely if half the town had been swept away by a tornado or vaporised by an alien space ship people wouldn't have taken the time to view the paintings displayed by the local art group.

Harvey handed Mrs Dalgetty a five pound note for a catalogue and waited patiently as she lifted various coins close to her face in search of the correct change.

"See, I told you not to worry," Harvey said as they walked around the main hall.

Claire looked at the tidily arranged artwork and listened to the buzz of conversation. It did all seem to be fine. As Mrs Dalgetty had said, several paintings already displayed small bright red dots indicating they'd been sold. There were none yet on Claire's but this was the first day of a week long event. There were none on Mrs Dalgetty's either, but there never would be. She hadn't painted for years, but still liked to be involved, so exhibited those of her paintings she hadn't wanted to part with.

By the end of the week, Claire had made two sales and no disasters had befallen anyone in Winkleigh Marsh.

Harvey helped with the dismantling of the exhibition. As they drove home, he said, "I noticed something about the paintings which sold."

"Oh?"

"They nearly all had people in. You sold your only two with figures in and, apart from a few flower studies, just about all the other sales had people somewhere. I know it's about more than just the money, but maybe you should think about adding them in where it's appropriate?"

Claire hesitated. "Maybe."

"I know you were a bit superstitious about that, but if anything the ones with figures were good luck."

"They seemed to be, yes."

"Trust me, Claire. Tell me what you're worried about."

There was really only one way to prove to her husband that this was more than a silly superstition on her part. "All right… At college I was madly in love and wanted to do a portrait of myself and my boyfriend. Of course I couldn't pose for it, so I got my flatmate to stand in for me. Before I'd got as far as painting in my features she'd moved out of our shared flat and into his."

"If your boyfriend left you for your friend, you were well rid of the pair of them, I'd say."

"Yes, probably, but there were other things… I did some experimental pictures of my family using odd colours. I made Dad red and my brother yellow. The paint wasn't even dry before Dad got horrible sunburn and soon after my brother developed jaundice and was diagnosed with hepatitis."

"That's quite a coincidence."

"There were other things. Models came to sit for us. I made a mess of the nose of one and as he left, somehow a door shut in his face and broke his nose."

"And was that the first time you'd ever made a mistake when painting a model's portrait?"

"No, of course not."

"And did everyone of the others injure that body part?"

"No, they didn't and you're starting to sound like everyone else I've ever told about this. They all say there were a couple of coincidences and once I was aware of them I started noticing or imagining more things."

"Maybe we're all right? But even if not, these things all happened years ago and any weird curse or whatever has clearly lost its power now."

Claire just shook her head.

They unloaded the paintings and carried them to Claire's studio.

"Why didn't you show that one?" Harvey asked, indicating a painting of Winkleigh Marsh High Street. "It's really good. I'm sure you'd have sold it, especially as it's got people in."

"Do you recognise them?"

"Hmm, yes. Mrs Dalgetty and that's poor old George, isn't it? Doesn't look quite right without his dog, does he?"

"No, he doesn't. His dog was alive when I painted this, Harvey. I tried to include the dog but messed up the scale, so took it out intending to try again when the paint, where the first attempt had been, was dry. The dog died that night."

"It was twenty-three years old, Claire. That's beyond ancient for a dog."

"Another coincidence?"

"Clearly."

"Then how about I paint you with a broken leg?"

"Wouldn't worry me." He didn't sound worried either, but he did look just a little nervous when he came into the studio ready to sit the following evening.

"You don't want to do this, do you?" Claire asked.

"I'm just worried that if I so much as trip on a paving slab you'll see it as proof that you're jinxed and if I go about worrying the whole time, I probably will manage to hurt myself."

Claire sighed in relief. "You're right. I won't do it then."

"You should, but I thought you could paint me with something nice happening."

"Oh. Yes… Yes, that might be OK. What though?" She began to sketch and, as always once she started work, became absorbed in what she was doing.

"As I am, would be fine really. I have a wonderful talented wife, a nice home. I'm in good health." Harvey continued to tell her how fortunate he considered himself, but eventually said, "I suppose I wouldn't actually complain if I had more money." He took the notes from his wallet and held them out for Claire to draw.

"OK, that's enough for today," she said twenty minutes later. "I can work on it tomorrow while you're at work."

Harvey won thirty-five pounds in the social club raffle that weekend.

"I've been short changed, love!" he teased Claire. "Fifty quid I showed you, two twenties and a ten."

"Come with me." She led him up to her studio and showed

him the portrait which had advanced considerably. In it the notes he was holding were a twenty, ten and a five. "I don't know why, but it seemed better to have them all different."

"OK, that is a bit odd," he admitted. "Not in a bad way though. I was saying how happy I am when you drew that. If you finish the painting maybe I'll stay that way forever?"

"I think you might," Claire said. It was worth trying, wasn't it? Painting was her passion and she knew she had a talent for it. Perhaps she also had a different kind of gift and just possibly she could learn not to fear it. Before she could lose her nerve, she leafed through their wedding album and made sketches of some of the guests, drawing them not exactly as they were in life, but a little more how she thought they would like to be. She slimmed cousin Betty's more than generous thighs, filled in uncle Robert's bald patch and seated her brother behind the wheel of a very smart looking car. She didn't stop until Harvey came to coax her into bed.

Claire enjoyed creating the detailed, realistic portrait of Harvey and wanted to do more. She did one of her parents-in-law, sitting in their garden. She took great care to make them look healthy and happy and for the garden to be full of glorious colour.

"That's lovely dear," they both said when they saw the result.

"Nice to see that rhododendron in flower too. Never has since we bought it," her father-in-law said. "Might as well get rid of it."

"Perhaps you should give it one more chance?" Harvey suggested. He winked at Claire.

It wasn't always easy to find people willing to sit still for her, but Claire knew someone who'd be willing; Mrs

Dalgetty. When Claire visited to ask, she was shocked to see how much the old lady had deteriorated since the art exhibition. Mrs Dalgetty had always dressed eccentrically, but her clothes were always clean. She was quite old, but she used to stride out purposefully wherever she was going. Her friendliness and hospitality were well known.

Now she looked unkempt and shuffled from the front door into her living room, saying, "If you want tea, perhaps you'd make it?"

She brightened when Claire did that, then asked if the lady would agree to have her portrait done.

"Yes I would, but unless you want to do it here, you'll have to come and fetch me. It's silly I know, but I don't like going out on my own these days."

"I'll do it here if that's OK. I think it would be nice to have some of your things around you."

As Claire worked, she learned that Mrs Dalgetty's sight had almost entirely gone. "One of the perks of growing old, my dear."

"Can't they do anything?" Claire asked.

"An operation was mentioned, but I'm frightened."

Who was Claire to tell someone not to give in to fear? She'd done just that for years.

"Mrs Dalgetty, would you mind posing with something, rather than just sitting?"

"Not at all, dear. It's a while since I've painted, but I do see that if I appeared to be doing something the picture will be more interesting. How about embroidery? There's some in that box there and if I remember rightly, the colours were rather nice."

Claire opened the box and took out an incomplete piece of

very intricate needlework. The greens and blues on cream cloth were just right to contrast with the deep red of Mrs Dalgetty's dress, the dark wood of her upright chair and her iron grey curls. "Oh yes, this would be perfect."

Carefully she placed the needle in Mrs Dalgetty's fingers and arranged the material so she appeared to be working. "Will you be too uncomfortable to stay like that while I make a sketch?"

"No… although I do wish I could work on this while you worked on the drawings."

Claire moved her pencil over the pad, only half listening to Mrs Dalgetty's talk of the difficulties her failing sight posed and her regret at the things she could no longer do. She concentrated mainly on getting the hands exactly right, so her model could relax them as soon as possible. The rest of Mrs Dalgetty was only roughly sketched in and her feet weren't drawn at all. The slippers she was wearing were scruffy and ugly. Of course Claire couldn't say so, but she could ask Mrs Dalgetty to wear different footwear for the next sitting. Due to various commitments of Claire's and a few things Mrs Dalgetty had scheduled, that wouldn't be for three weeks.

Two days beforehand Claire received a message. Mrs Dalgetty was sorry to inconvenience her, but wouldn't be able to keep her appointment as she was in hospital.

"That poor woman!" Claire wailed. "What have I done to her?"

"You haven't done anything," Harvey tried to reassure her.

"Look at the drawing. She doesn't have any feet. She must have fallen …"

"If she has it's because she can't see. You said yourself she rarely goes out for fear of that, but maybe it's nothing to do with her feet?"

Claire wasn't listening. "Look at these." She pulled out the file of sketches she'd made from their wedding album. "Everyone we care about is here. What can I do, Harvey? What can I do?"

He was saved from answering by the ringing of Claire's phone. She just about recognised her sister's voice through the sobs, but could make no sense of what she was saying.

"Laura, stop! Now take a couple of deep breaths." She waited. "OK, now tell me what's wrong."

Laura shrieked in her ear.

"Pregnant? Did you say pregnant?" Claire asked.

Harvey lifted the sketch of Laura holding the baby she'd always longed for and handed it to Claire. He kissed her cheek and slipped from the room.

Laura told her she hadn't dared to believe it at first, but the doctor had confirmed it and she'd just had a scan showing everything was fine.

"There doesn't seem to be any reason why I can't hope to have a healthy baby in my arms in six month's time."

Claire looked at the sketch she'd made three months previously. "You will do, Laura. I'm sure you will."

Harvey came back. "Good news."

"The best! Did you hear? Laura is pregnant at last."

"I gathered. Is everything… I mean…"

"Yes. She should be OK. Apparently her problems conceiving shouldn't make any difference to the pregnancy."

"Mrs Dalgetty is OK too. I phoned round and apparently she's finally given in to the coaxing of her family and doctor and agreed to have the operation on her eyes. Because she had private medical insurance and was available any time, she was able to have it done almost immediately."

Claire was soon able to continue with her portrait of Mrs Dalgetty. By the time it was finished, the elderly lady was again wearing spotlessly clean clothes and walked purposefully when she got up to brew tea and cut freshly baked cake. Other than that she sat quietly, working on her needlework, as Claire painted.

Next she set to work bringing to life the sketches she'd made of family and friends. Uncle Robert's hair continued to recede in defiance of the efforts Claire made with her paints, but Cousin Betty fell in love with a marathon runner. Cycling alongside him on his training runs whittled her plump figure down to a neat size 14. Claire's brother didn't suddenly buy a new car but nothing bad happened to his old one either. Their other friends and family had the usual mix of good and bad luck. Sometimes, if Claire looked closely, she could see hints of that in the paintings. She worked too on a painting of Laura and the baby, adding to it gradually with great care.

"Have you decided if you'll make the blanket pink or blue?" Harvey asked.

She grinned. "I'm doing it lemon. There's only so much responsibility I'm willing to accept."

"So you aren't worried about your supernatural powers any more?"

"No, that was just silly superstition."

Harvey nodded. "Shall I start loading up the ones you're taking to the exhibition?"

"Ummm… You'll have to help me put the frames back on

first."

"Why did you take them off?"

"No reason really."

If Harvey noticed the still wet, brilliant red dots she'd added to the corner of each picture, he tactfully didn't say. Once the frames were back on they wouldn't show. He wasn't at all surprised when every single painting sold; his wife was a very talented artist.

8. Lie Detector Locket

Everyone knew it was no use lying to Gran. Not that Elspeth usually wanted to, but sometimes she'd said things which were untrue. Little things such as she didn't know how the flower vase got broken, despite the fact she'd knocked it over when skipping indoors after being told not to. Or claiming not to have had her tea yet if she knew Gran had been baking. Gran had always known, but she'd still cut her a generous wedge of cake.

As a teenager Elspeth became moody and withdrawn. She claimed to hate both her silly old-fashioned name as well as the parents who'd given it to her. Gran had intervened and asked Elspeth to stay with her for a few days.

She'd enjoyed what felt like a return to a trouble free childhood. Gran had baked her delicious cakes and got Elspeth to help do up her silver locket just as she'd done so many times before.

"You tell your old Gran what's wrong," she'd said.

"Nothing," Elspeth muttered, just as she did when her parents asked the same thing.

Gran had seen through that straight away and got to the truth which was that Elspeth was being bullied. Once it was admitted it was fairly soon sorted out.

When Elspeth got engaged to a man she knew her parents were struggling to like Gran gave her the locket and put it on her. Something seemed wrong about that. Oh yes, that was it. Whenever the locket had come out before, Gran always asked someone to fasten it for her. Elspeth thought that was because the catch was so fiddly but now, years later, Gran managed easily despite a touch of arthritis.

"I've not told anyone about the locket before, no one except your Granddad."

"I've seen it lots of times, Gran."

"Yes, but you don't know anything about it, do you?"

That was true. Gran always told the truth and there was never an explanation about the fastening of the locket. Of course putting it on someone else was different from trying to do it up around your own neck.

"One and one is two," Gran said.

"Of course it is." Elspeth hoped this wasn't going to be a talk about how babies were made.

"Two and two is ninety four."

Elspeth felt a jolt of pain. "Ouch! Something bit me!"

"What sort of something, love?"

"I don't know." She rubbed her throat, but other than the locket there was nothing there.

"The moon is made of green cheese," Gran declared.

The pain was back. Well, perhaps not pain exactly, more of a hot feeling just where the locket touched her skin.

"What you felt was the heat of a lie."

"That doesn't make any sense."

"Maybe not, but it's the truth."

Elspeth didn't say anything. How do you break it to your beloved Grandmother that her bag of marbles has burst and they're rolling all over the floor?

"I don't know how it works, or why, but if the person who fastens it around your neck lies to you, the locket heats up," Gran said.

"That's how you've always known if we weren't telling the truth?"

"Partly. I think we're all better at detecting lies than we give ourselves credit for, it's just that sometimes we don't want to believe those we care about aren't being honest."

"I suppose you could be right." It wasn't a comforting thought.

"I want you to have it, love, and I'd like you to ask that young man of yours to fasten it for you."

"You don't like him much, do you?"

"I don't altogether trust him."

"So you're hoping I'll catch him lying to me?"

"No, love. I'm hoping you'll discover I'm mistaken. I could be couldn't I?"

"Of course you are. Jim loves me and we're going to get married and he …"

"So ask him to fasten the locket around your neck, where could be the harm be in that?"

Elspeth didn't have an answer and the locket was beautiful. She'd always liked it.

A few days later she'd convinced herself that she'd imagined the hot feeling and that Gran had just wanted her to have the heirloom as an engagement present. Or maybe it was to put to rest the concerns of her family. Yes, that could be it. If Elspeth reported to Gran that she'd worn the locket as requested and was reassured Jim was entirely trustworthy, then Gran would pass that on and they'd properly accept him.

It didn't work out as planned. The locket sent out bursts of heat so often Elspeth was surprised not to see scorch marks on her neck. Jim's position at work and therefore salary were lower than he implied. He'd not given his car to a friend, it had been repossessed. His occasional quick drink with friends were long binges with people he hardly knew.

Elspeth had a good job, they'd manage perfectly well on the wages he was really earning. Together they could clear his debts and she could support him as he got help with his drinking, but only if he was honest about it all.

As she called Jim on small untruths he compounded them with bigger lies. He didn't trust her enough to be honest and she couldn't trust him enough to get married. Knowing that didn't stop her being miserable when they split up, but perhaps it had saved her from even greater unhappiness later on.

After that she didn't wear the locket for a long, long time. For one thing it now held that unhappy memory. For another she didn't need it. Gran had been right; generally she could tell if someone was telling her the truth. She'd had doubts about Jim she now realised, but hadn't wanted to face them. She'd been out with other men since, but she'd never asked them to fasten the locket around her neck. Until Daniel they'd not been important enough for their honesty to really matter. Daniel was important, but she trusted him.

"You've not worn the locket lately, love," Gran said.

Elspeth explained why not.

"I'm glad. You might wear it for your wedding though. I wore it at mine."

"You don't think I should wear it before and check I'm doing the right thing?"

"Go and fetch it."

When Elspeth returned with it, Gran did it up for her.

"I suggested you wear it just because it's beautiful and it could be your something old to bring you luck."

The locket remained cool against her skin and Elspeth knew she didn't need to fear asking Daniel to fasten it for her. She didn't need to fear asking, or telling, him anything.

"My Gran gave it to me," she said. "It reveals if a person is telling the truth."

"Let me put it on for you then. I want to find out if you're too good to be true!" He took the locket from her and fastened it around her neck. "OK now tell me; do you love me and will we be happy forever?"

"Yes I do and yes we will."

"I know you do, because I love you too." He kissed her then and she never did get around to explaining that wasn't how the locket worked.

Elspeth wore it for her wedding, but took it off just before they left for honeymoon and asked her Gran to keep it safe. "I don't think I need it any more, but that doesn't mean I'm prepared to risk losing it."

The locket came out for special occasions. If Daniel was in the room when she took it from her jewellery box he did it up for her. Sometimes she fastened it herself. Either way, no matter what her husband told her, it never became hot. One day, not long after their twenty-third anniversary she wished it would.

"I'm worried about Skye. There's something really wrong with our daughter," Daniel said.

Elspeth felt cold. Not just because the locket he'd put round her neck before they'd gone out for the evening was failing to heat up, but because he was voicing the thought she'd been trying not to accept.

"She says she's fine," Elspeth says.

"I know. Can you try talking to her again?"

"Yes, I'll try."

That weekend Elspeth asked Skye to check the catch on the locket. "It doesn't feel right." That was true. She got Daniel to hook it through the lace of her blouse when he put it on for her just before Skye arrived.

"It's all tangled up, Mum." Skye undid, untangled and refastened the locket.

"Thanks, love. Now come and tell your Mum what's wrong."

"Nothing."

The locket was momentarily red hot. After a few more questions and as many evasive answers Elspeth had a good idea what was wrong. If she was right it was worse than her own trouble with Jim had been. Worse than Elspeth and Daniel had feared, but not completely hopeless, not if the three of them were honest and worked together.

Elspeth undid the locket and beckoned her daughter forward.

"Don't give it to me, Mum."

Elspeth guessed that's because though she might not really want to, Skye knew she'd soon sell it. In a way that was encouraging. Skye was at least admitting some of the truth to herself.

"Just wear it for a little while then. There's something I want to show you."

Elspeth did the locket up around her daughter's too thin

neck.

"We love you Skye, your dad and I and we'll help you."

"I don't need any help."

"Look at me love."

Skye complied.

"You are absolutely fine."

"Ouch!" Skye rubbed her throat.

"The locket got hot, didn't it?"

"Yes."

"What you felt was the heat of a lie. I felt it when you said you were OK, that Jake was looking after you, that the police had made a mistake."

"Oh, Mum."

"There's nothing anyone can do to help you."

"Ouch!"

"Another lie, you see?"

"That doesn't make any sense. An old locket can't tell if someone is lying."

"The Beatles are getting back together, there are no calories in pizza, one swallow makes a summer."

"Stop it, Mum. It hurts."

"Then let's try this. I'm not happy you've lied to us and we're disappointed about some of the things you've done."

Skye sniffed. "That hurts too," she whispered.

"Is the locket hot?"

"No. You're telling the truth and you're right to be angry. I'm no good and ..."

"Now you stop it." She hugged her daughter. "I'm not angry. Sad yes, but not angry. And yes, you've done some bad things but you're not a bad person."

"Really?"

"What do you think?"

"I think you mean it."

"Your dad and I love you, Skye. If you're honest with us we can help you. It isn't going to be easy, but we can sort out some of the immediate problems and work with you to figure out the rest."

"I should never have lied to you."

"No, there's never any sense in lying to those you love, but that's in the past now."

Skye removed the locket and put in back on Elspeth.

"And the future starts now, Mum. I'm ready for it."

Elspeth's locket grew hot.

"No that's not true, I'm not ready at all," Skye admitted. "My life is a mess. Jake doesn't care about me at all, he doesn't care about anything except his next fix and I'm not much better."

Elspeth searched through the leaflets she'd collected, on every problem she'd feared her daughter might be facing, and handed her the one which seemed most appropriate. "Are you at least ready to ask for help and to try to accept it and work towards a future?"

Skye read through the information, then pointing at the phone number printed on every page asked, "Can I borrow your phone?" She dialled. "Hi… Yes, um I think you might be able to help me."

Elspeth felt a warm glow. It wasn't from the locket, that stayed cool against her skin. What Elspeth felt was love and hope.

9. The Thing In Her Head

Sonia was tired after yet another disturbed night. She knew why, it was all down to her job. The agency gave it a fancy title, but really she was a medically trained home help; part nurse, part cleaner, part anything else the client wanted and she could do in a two hour slot. Most of her clients were lovely, a real pleasure to be around despite their difficulties. Not Harry though. Being near that miserable old so and so would make anyone dream about committing murder!

At least, it could all be Harry's fault. She hoped so.

Nothing was ever right for Harry, and Sonia took the blame. For instance she knew he could get up and dress unaided, but on the days she was due he stayed in bed until she arrived. In just under a year, she'd been late three times, once when her car broke down and twice because previous clients had serious medical problems. On all three occasions he'd wet the bed, meaning she had to deal with that, staying longer than she was paid for, to get everything done.

She took him the free newspaper as she did for her other clients who wanted it. Harry held her responsible for any headlines he took exception to. Apparently it was part of a her job to send all the immigrants home, lower gas prices and make people realise zombies were no laughing matter.

"When people are dead they stay dead!" he'd yelled.

Sonia certainly hoped so. Harry was bad enough alive and she couldn't honestly say she'd mind if he didn't stay that way much longer. She'd had her first bad dream that night. One of the undead came for Harry and, just as he kept saying, she did nothing to help him.

The thing in her head seemed to agree with her when she wanted to push him out the windows he was always demanding she open or close. She'd never lift him up there though, even if he didn't struggle and she knew he would. Shooting him would be good, but she didn't have a gun and had no idea where to get one. A lethal injection was appealing, but she no longer had access to the kind of medications which would do the job.

Every night in her sleep she did horrible things which she'd never do for real. She didn't want to, really she didn't. Harry deserved it though, didn't he? She should kill him really. It would be for the best.

Harry complained he was too hot then, when she'd gone, rang her boss and said she'd left him to freeze with the heating off and every window open. Fortunately previous staff members had experienced similar things and Sonia's boss had done no more than given her a warning to be more careful.

Then Harry accused her of stealing one of his watches.

"It's not fair," she told her husband. "His place is full of all kinds of old watches and little metal boxes, which he keeps hiding and then losing. He probably knows I didn't take it, but that won't stop him reporting it."

"Don't worry, you can't get into trouble without proof," Alex, a policeman, assured her.

"No, I suppose not, but it makes me angry that he's saying it. Does he think I'm stupid? Some of his things probably are antique and valuable but I wouldn't want to steal them. They're too distinctive. It would be impossible to move them on."

"What did you say?" Alex asked.

What had she said? She had a headache and couldn't think straight. "I wouldn't steal them because I'm not a thief."

"Of course you're not, love."

"Don't take that patronising tone with me! You don't trust me either, do you? Of course you wouldn't, being a copper."

"Sonia, what's wrong?" He caught her as her body sagged. "Is it your headaches? They've come back?"

She nodded. Even that hurt. Alex helped her to bed, closed the curtains and laid a cool flannel on her forehead. The poor man looked so worried. That's why she hadn't told him they'd been back for some time. That and the hope she had them under control at last. The latest tablets from the doctor did seem to help a bit.

The headaches had started when she was quite young. They hurt but that wasn't the worst part. They gave her a feeling of not being in control of her life. Sometimes it felt as though there was someone or something else inside her head flipping switches. Sometimes when she was in a shop her head would ache and she'd want to grab a handful of sweets and stuff them in her pocket. She silenced that thought by concentrating on the bad things which would happen if she were caught. The thing in her head didn't bother her for quite a while.

As a teenager Sonia experienced headaches whenever she was near one particular boy. It was just a slight buzz at first, quickly gone if she moved away from him, but becoming disorientatingly painful if not. He was clearly interested in her and she liked him too, but the thing going on in her head made sure she kept her distance. When the boy, and passenger on his moped, were injured it seemed she'd had a lucky escape.

The headaches didn't return until she was old enough to leave school and take a job. It seemed that's what the thing in her head wanted her to do, but she'd resisted and stayed on to get the qualifications she'd need to become a nurse. The headaches she got while studying left her too tired to do much else. Her social life was zero. They stopped though the moment she put down her pen at the end of her final exam.

Whatever the thing was, it hadn't wanted her to move away from home to train. Sonia was determined. The struggle gave her more headaches but they went once she'd accepted the course and it was too late to apply for one closer. Knowing the thing gave up once it was beaten gave her a measure of power.

She knew it disliked Alex. Sonia didn't though. She'd had to tell him about the headaches to explain the way her mood seemed to change and how sometimes when he was close they left her almost too weak to stand.

"Lean on me then, Sonia. I'll always be here to support you."

"Always?"

"If you'll let me."

The headaches grew worse right up until he proposed. By then they were so bad she had trouble focussing on his face and doubted she had the strength to accept. The moment she forced out a feeble 'yes' her head cleared. Sonia remained pain free through the wedding, the honeymoon and for years afterwards. It seemed as though the thing in her head had switched itself off.

Even so when Mum suggested she and Alex move in with her she'd worried it wouldn't just be her husband's wishes to be taken into account.

"I could look after Mum so she doesn't have to leave her home. I doubt she'd accept any rent, but if we paid all the bills that would help her and still save us money. It's practical and… I would like to do it."

"Financially it makes enormous sense and you know I've always got on with your mum. If we can arrange it so we get some time to ourselves, I think it's a good idea."

Sonia had braced herself for a jolt of pain. The thing in her head hadn't wanted her to move before, but it seemed to be raising no objections now. Had it really gone, or did it approve of her returning to the town where she'd been born?

The same thing had happened, or rather not happened, when she'd seen the job advert. It wasn't what she'd done before but it would suit her new circumstances and made use of her medical training. She'd had a weird feeling just for a moment and was sure the thing in her head had an opinion, but no headaches had come. At least not until miserable old Harry had been added to her client list. He was a pain, but in a different way.

She'd disliked him right from the start. Really disliked him. That was unusual. Throughout her career as a nurse and now as a home help she'd met many people who were unhappy, rude or unpleasant. Sonia knew that often it was because they were in pain, ill or frightened either about their own future or that of a loved one. As she helped them and got to know them, their true characters were revealed to be far nicer than they'd seemed initially. Not so with Harry. She'd yet to find a single redeeming feature.

He seemed to feel the same way about her, often shouting at her and calling her worthless. Sonia knew she wasn't. Her other clients, even the grumpy ones, thanked her occasionally at least and many said how much her visits helped them.

Before her fortieth birthday she'd asked some clients if she could reschedule her visits to keep that day clear.

"November the second? That's all Soul's day isn't it, dear?" one lady asked.

"Yes." The day for remembering the dead, or the time when the dead return, depending on your point of view. She'd had some teasing at school over it.

"That's no problem, then. My daughter always takes me to my husband's and parents' graves that day. I'll ask her to come earlier so she can help me get up. Do you have far to go?" She placed a hand on Sonia's arm as though offering sympathy.

Sonia hadn't said it was her birthday as she didn't want her clients to feel obliged to give her a gift, but did so then.

"Oh! You have a nice time then. Will you have a party? I had a lovely party when I was about your age." She prattled on for the rest of the visit, sharing happy memories.

All Sonia's other clients agreed to the change just as readily. Every one but Harry.

"And just what am I supposed to do if you're too lazy to come, you useless girl?"

Sonia's head hurt and she lost her temper. "If I'm useless you won't miss me, will you? You can just sit here all alone and think about what happened forty years ago to the day. Do you think about it Harry?" Both her words and voice sounded odd to Sonia.

Harry's reaction was even odder. He looked scared. "Don't you threaten me! Don't you dare threaten me!"

For her next few visits Harry was very subdued. Not pleasant or polite or anything, but he didn't shout at her or go out of his way to be difficult. The change was temporary though and she continued to fantasise about getting rid of him.

Sonia didn't tell Alex about the dreams, especially not that although she knew they were nightmares and horrible, they felt like dreams. Killing Harry felt good. That's why she had so much trouble sleeping. She didn't tell him either about the sleeping tablets she'd persuaded her doctor to prescribe. How she took them into work with her and thought about putting them all in Harry's tea. The thing in her head wanted her to. Her head hurt so much when she added only milk and sugar that she knew she couldn't carry it in to him without spilling it.

"Hurry up, you stupid girl!" Harry yelled.

'Yes, hurry up,' her head told her. 'Kill him and it will all be over.'

Sonia crawled to the bathroom and flushed the tablets down the toilet. Only then did her headache clear. Even without it she had a hard job ignoring Harry's horrible comments when she eventually took in his perfectly safe drink.

There was no one she could tell. Not her boss who'd rightly not want staff members with murderous desires. Not her mother who now relied on her care. Not her policeman husband. She did tell Alex when Harry threw a mug at her, bruising her ear.

"Don't go back," Alex suggested. "Either say you won't go back to Harry's or pack in your job altogether. We don't really need the money now."

"No. I won't let him beat me, Alex."

"It's not about that, it's about you being happy and you're

not."

Would she be any happier if she stayed away from Harry? The thing in her head had made it clear he wanted him dead, but if Sonia gave in her notice perhaps it would accept defeat and leave her alone? She picked up the phone to call her boss. Immediately her head began to swim. It cleared again as soon as she hung up.

"I can't do it over the phone," she said. "I'm not sure I can do it at all. Alex, this is going to sound very weird, but ..." She told him part of the story. About how it sometimes felt as though someone or something was inside her head controlling her thoughts and that going against its wishes gave her the headaches.

"You're right, it does sound weird, but your headaches are weird too. If we can work out what's going on maybe we can stop it."

"Maybe." She thought he was just humouring her, but she'd wanted to tell someone for so long that she couldn't stop now. "Looking back, I think it's manipulated me into a position in which I'd come into contact with Harry. It's been trying all along I think. First to keep me here then, when that didn't work, to bring me back. "

"So do you think whatever it is is a friend of Harry's? It wants to stay near him through you?"

"No, definitely not. Harry seems frightened." She remembered how he'd reacted when she'd spoken the thing's words. "Alex, I think it's all connected to my birthday."

"We could look at records from that time, see if anything unusual happened then."

"You believe me then? You don't think I'm crazy?"

"No, I don't think that. I'm wondering if you saw

something terrifying when you were a child and suppressed it. I've come across that sometimes. A witness is so traumatised they block it all out and only gradually remember."

"But this has been going on all my life."

"The headaches and migraines could be flashbacks. Something triggers them and Harry is the biggest trigger of all."

"So, where do we look?"

"The library will have old newspapers and things. We could start there. Begin at your birth and work forward."

"Good idea." The thing in her head thought so too.

At Alex's suggestion they started with the local paper, which meant they didn't have to search for long. At the time she was born, and in the same hospital, someone had died. The man warranted a mention in the paper because he'd been a burglar. His unconscious body was found at the scene of a break in. The valuable collection of watches, snuff boxes and other small items was missing. Police assumed there had been two thieves and one had hit the other over the head with a blunt instrument before taking all the loot. The unconscious man never recovered and his murderous colleague and the stolen goods were never located.

"It was Harry! Harry killed him," Sonia said.

"I suppose that's one possibility. From what you've said he sounds capable of it."

"It's true, Alex. I know it is." She now also knew the identity of the thing in her head. According to the newspaper he had once been Frederick 'Fingers' French. No wonder she'd sometimes had the urge to steal things and wanted to harm Harry. That Frederick hadn't wanted her to move away from his intended victim, nor to have a relationship with another man, also made sense. At least it did to her, she doubted anyone else would be so sure. "I know, Alex. I just do."

"Then how do we prove it? The inspector will need more to go on than what we can tell him."

"Of course he will." And of course Alex didn't want to attempt to use his wife's headaches as evidence. "Harry seemed scared when I told him to think back forty years. I think if I confront him on my birthday he'll tell me the truth."

"If he does you'll need witnesses. I can arrange that."

On November the second Sonia let herself, Alex and detective sergeant Marks into Harry's flat.

Harry called out his usual greeting of, "Is that you, you useless girl? You're late!"

"Forty years too late," she couldn't stop herself saying. The weird feeling was there, but no pain.

"What did you say?" Harry screamed.

Alex gave her a warning look. He'd told her to be careful not to do or say anything which might jeopardise a court case.

Sonia took a deep breath and walked through to Harry's bedroom. "Harry, I'm not late and I'm not alone. There's someone here who'd like to talk to you about something which happened exactly forty years ago. Will you talk to him?"

Harry hauled himself into a sitting position and pulled the blankets around himself. "No I won't! You've no right bringing someone in here. No right." His face was a blotchy combination of anger and fear.

She'd informed him the detective was there and Harry hadn't insisted he leave. Hopefully that would be enough to allow him to use anything he heard as evidence. Now all she had to do was persuade Harry to talk.

"It's dark in here, why don't I draw the curtains for you?" she asked brightly.

Harry nodded agreement. That wasn't like him, normally he'd have snapped that she should have done it already.

As Sonia stepped in front of the window she knew she'd appear as a silhouette to Harry. "Do you know what day it is, Harry?" she said quietly. Her voice sounded unusually low.

Harry seemed to shrink in on himself and the splotches of red vanished from his face. "Just another day. It means nothing to me." The words came as a croaky whisper.

Sonia pulled one curtain open. The low winter sunlight made her blink, but it didn't hurt her head. She reached out for the other curtain and as she did the shadow of her hand appeared to leap up the bed towards Harry.

"Not Fingers. Don't let him near me! He should be dead. I killed him, why isn't he dead?" Harry screamed.

Alex and his sergeant raced in and told Harry he had the right to remain silent. He didn't want it, he wanted to talk and to be taken somewhere Frederick couldn't reach him.

Sonia doubted there was such a place, because her head felt lighter and freer than it had ever done.

10. Office Angel

"Son, hire someone like Mrs Highmore, if you possibly can." That was Dad's final piece of advice as he handed over the company. Advice Gary had no intention of taking; he hated being manipulated.

He remembered Dad's secretary from when he worked in the office during college holidays. She'd been a terror. No chance of skiving or using the company phone to call his girlfriends. Staff grumbled she haunted the stationery cupboard, making it impossible to help themselves to as much as a pencil.

Gary hadn't been bothered about the lack of pilfering opportunities, but had wondered why Dad hadn't employed someone a bit more glamorous and friendly. Mrs Highmore stayed on long after the age of sixty-five, unusual in those days, but Dad had been happy to keep her on as long as she wanted to stay.

Gary's own secretary was in a very different class. Mandi, 'with an i', she'd explained at the interview giving a saucy wink, was much younger than Gary. She was very pretty and not at all terrifying. Actually Mandi seemed very keen to please him, unlike his wife Jane of late.

Coincidentally not long after Mandi started, the company ran into financial trouble. Jane seemed to blame him for not maintaining proper control rather than realising times were tough for everyone.

Jane said, "Costs have skyrocketed. Stationery alone has

quadrupled since you took over, despite everything being computerised now. Wages are higher, yet output is down. You're letting staff take advantage. You need a proper office manager."

"I've got one!"

"Mandi is no Mrs Highmore."

Gary was glad of that.

Jane had always done Gary's accounts for him, just like Mrs Highmore had for Dad, except Jane used to work from home. She started coming in more often, demanding he look over the books or approve tax returns. That meant far fewer business lunches with Mandi.

His personal assistant, as Mandi liked to be known, wasn't exactly happy about that but only on his account. "You work so hard. You should get some reward, relax a little."

Mandi was giving him a massage when Jane arrived unexpectedly one afternoon. It was perfectly innocent, but Mandi could have been a bit more tactful about it. There was no need for her to leap away from him and start adjusting her clothing like that. Gary could almost understand Jane getting the wrong idea.

"Your dad was right," she snapped as soon as Mandi scurried out. "He warned you to employ someone like …"

"Like the angelic Mrs Highmore?" Gary interrupted. "What do you want me to do? Summon her up from the dead?" He chanted her name three times.

Jane ignored that and said, "You know the charity she left her money to?"

"Not precisely." He'd not taken any notice of anything to do with Mrs Highmore after she retired, although his parents had kept in touch.

"It provides pens and books to very poor children in third world countries so they can get some kind of education. Your father set up a small standing order to it, almost as though she were still on the payroll, when she left. I think we should start it again."

"Why would we want to do that?"

"Because it's a good thing to do and would please your father. Besides charity donations are tax deductible and if you were to control yourself better you'd save more than it costs."

There was something about the way she mentioned controlling himself Gary didn't like, almost as though she wasn't talking in strictly business terms.

"Go on then, if you must."

Jane had the payment set up in minutes. It took Mandi all day to amend a payment to any of their suppliers. Obviously Jane had this planned in advance and waited until she thought she'd caught him at a disadvantage. Was everyone trying to push him into doing things?

Not long after Jane left, there was something else for Gary to deal with. The cupboard to the stationery cupboard jammed with Mandi stuck inside. One of the young men from dispatch had to force it open. Why he'd been in there to start with Gary had no idea, but it was a good job he was.

Gary sent Mandi home early to help her get over the trauma, then ordered a sign be put up warning people not to shut the door until it had been checked. Why anyone ever did Gary couldn't imagine. The stationery cupboard wasn't well lit, he himself had to keep the door wide open just so he could find whatever he needed.

The following morning over breakfast he just happened to

mention the incident. He'd thought Jane, who was slightly claustrophobic, would be sympathetic over Mandi's ordeal, but she'd seemed to find it hilarious. Gary went into work earlier than usual.

As he passed the stationery cupboard he noticed the closed door. When he pulled it open he caught a member of staff stuffing a rucksack with pens, correction fluid and notebooks. She tearfully claimed her children needed it for school and pleaded with him to be lenient.

Gary, mesmerised by the way her cleavage trembled with every sob, almost forgave her. That was until Mandi arrived and informed him the thief had only just returned from maternity leave for her first child. Gary was forced to dismiss the woman.

After that difficult incident Mandi massaged his tense shoulder muscles.

"Oh, that's wonderful," Gary murmured.

"I could do a much better job if you were to lie down."

"I can't."

"Not here, but if you came to my place tomorrow …"

Gary gave her the day off work as she said she'd need time to prepare. She also managed to work in a hint about how much she loved flowers and champagne.

Gary ordered flowers to be delivered to Mandi. He couldn't risk being seen with them.

"Of course, sir. To Bayswater Drive?"

It was so long since he'd ordered flowers for Jane he'd forgotten the florist knew his home address. "Er no, not this time." Gary gave Mandi's address.

Mandi was dressed even more alluringly than usual when she opened her door and accepted the bottle he'd bought on the way.

"You look beautiful," he told her.

"As pretty as a flower?"

"Yes …" He noticed her pout and the lack of blooms in her flat. "I ordered some to be delivered this afternoon."

"Oh, but I was in the salon."

He'd imagined she'd be cooking for him. Jane spent hours preparing when she cooked him a special meal.

As Mandi had spent the time getting pampered he supposed she'd spent the money he'd given her on ready prepared food. "What are we eating?" he asked.

"You can choose where to take me …afterwards."

Gary studied Mandi carefully. Yes, she was gorgeous on the outside but, just like her apparent concern for him, it was all superficial. He'd compared Jane unfavourably with this girl, but he'd been wrong to do so. His wife didn't have time to go to the salon for hours, as she looked after him, their children and home as well as doing the company's accounts. Something which should really be Mandi's job. He realised what a terrible mistake he'd been making and that he'd been about to make it much worse.

As he rushed home to Jane, Gary vowed to be a far better husband in future. He'd start by replacing Mandi with someone efficient so Jane didn't need to work so hard, nor worry about him losing control of the company or himself.

Jane looked up from her computer and smiled as he walked into the lounge. She hadn't done that recently, he'd forgotten how pretty it made her look.

"Almost finished the pay run. Dinner is nearly ready, but you've got time to change if you want to."

He'd been so selfish and thoughtless he'd not even told her

he might be late back! "Can I do anything to help?" he asked. "Or pour you a drink?"

"It's all under control, but yes please to the drink."

As he headed for the kitchen she called, "Thank you for the flowers. I'll arrange them properly in a minute."

He saw a huge bouquet, just like the one he'd tried to send Mandi, in the sink. When they couldn't be delivered to her, the florist must have brought them to his home. If Jane had seen Mandi's name on the card…

"I'm glad they arrived all right," he said as he carried the drinks in to Jane.

"It's odd, but the lady who brought them looked just as I remember Mrs Highmore. Obviously she's not as efficient though, as she'd lost the card!"

Gary wasn't so sure. Dad had said someone like Mrs Highmore would always look after both his, and the company's, interests and Gary was beginning to believe it.

11. Baby Shoes

"Want to go in there, do you?"

I didn't like my stepdaughter's tone but I turned to look where she pointed. It was a mother and baby shop. If she'd punched me it would have hurt less. She knows of course that I can't have a baby. It's something I shared with her, back when we shared confidences. We used to share so much. We haven't been getting on so well lately, or at all really, but never before had Chrissie been cruel. In fact I'd had hopes today that things were getting better.

Mum, who was in the mall's toilets, had asked her to come with us on this shopping trip.

"It won't be the same without my lovely granddaughter to spoil," she'd coaxed. Chrissie soon gave in, despite the fact she'd snapped, "No chance," when I'd asked her. To be fair, I'm sure it was because she saw Mum really wanted her to come, not just because she knew she'd be bought a few nice things. She's a good kid really. That's why her words and attitude recently have hurt me so much. Saying something mean like that was so unlike her it had to be calculated cruelty and not just a bout of petulance.

"Why are you being like this, Chrissie?"

"Me? You're the one pushing me away."

"That's so not true." It wasn't. I love her and it distressed me to see her as unhappy as she'd been lately.

"Yeah, right."

Fortunately Mum came back then. Her bright smile faded as she reached us. At first I thought it was because she'd picked up on our row but she too pointed at the mother and baby shop.

"Oh, Laura, will you look at that."

What was this, a conspiracy? "I've seen it Mum."

"What does it mean?" Chrissie asked.

"It doesn't mean anything, it's just a shop."

Mum went pale and held out a shaking hand. "All those shoes."

I looked properly and saw dozens of pairs of baby shoes, booties and sandals arranged in the shape of one bigger shoe.

Mum sagged, caught just in time by me and Chrissie.

"All those shoes, Laura," Mum murmured as though in a trance.

Great. Just what I needed; Mum having one of her premonitions. She's got this weird thing where every now and then she'll see a baby shoe and go all 'ghost of Christmas yet to come' on me.

"Should we get her some water or sweet tea or something?" Chrissie asked.

"Tea is a good idea. Let's get her into the coffee shop."

We walked her over there. Mum co-operated but leaned heavily on us both.

I saw how worried Chrissie looked and tried to reassure her. "She'll be OK soon, she's done this before."

We got Mum into a chair and I sent Chrissie to order a big pot of tea and a selection of cakes.

"Shall I ask them to call a doctor or anything?"

"No, tea will sort her out, honestly."

She nodded and went to do as I'd asked, all trace of her previous sullenness gone. As I said, she's a good kid really. I used to think that I'd found the child I'd always wanted in my stepdaughter. We'd got on well right from our first meeting. People had warned me it would take her a while to come round but it hadn't. Maybe it helped that she'd been with her dad when I met him so she felt part of our relationship, not threatened by it. Chrissie had been eleven then and we'd become an almost instant family; me, her and Stewart.

I was determined not to demand a place in her life where I wasn't wanted but Chrissie was happy for me to do all the mother stuff. It was me she told when her periods started and me who went with her when she was fitted for her first bra. She even told me about the crush she had on a boy at school. Chrissie's mother had never wanted a baby and had as little to do with her as possible, so she wasn't much competition, but I know Chrissie loved me for myself. Loved past tense. She'd been distant for a while.

Mum started to recover. "Did you see all those shoes?"

"Yes, Mum."

"What do they mean?"

"Nothing. They never do. It's all your imagination."

Chrissie carried over the tray just then. I could tell she was relieved to see Mum looking better.

Mum must have realised too, because she said, "Sorry I scared you."

"What was it, Gran?"

"Sometimes when I see baby shoes I get a funny feeling and know something is going to happen."

"But it doesn't Mum, I can prove it." I told her how I met Stewart when we were both buying children's shoes. Mine were indeed baby booties for my little sister's new baby. Stewart was with Chrissie buying her first pair for secondary school. "I never told you that, Mum because I knew you'd take against him if I had."

"I certainly wouldn't have! And anyway the fact that a baby shoe lead to you meeting him proves my point."

"How can you say that? Stewart is a wonderful husband and …"

"Exactly! And look at the terrible men you'd dated before."

"Oooh tell me about all her terrible boyfriends," Chrissie asked, just like her old self.

We used to tease each other all the time. Before I married her dad, I showed her photos of the frilliest puce bridesmaid dresses I could find and pretended I had my heart set on her wearing something like it. In turn she'd shown me skimpy black numbers that could probably be best described as slutty-goth. In the end she'd worn a dusky pink satin shift that we'd both loved.

"Oh go on, Mum tell her. Maybe she can learn from my mistakes," I said. What I really hoped was that hearing about them would bring us closer again.

"The worst one was Zack or something silly like that. He was just plain horrible, but of course Laura didn't see past the bad boy charm. One day he turned up with what looked like a baby trapped in the boot of his car. Really it was just a stuffed sock and baby's shoe hanging out, but it looked horrible. When he laughed at the shocked look on our neighbour's face I realised he was a thoroughly nasty piece of work."

I too had found it distasteful but had pretended I thought it was funny as I'd been so besotted with him. Mum had one of her turns when she saw it and begged me to finish with him. I didn't, not then. Soon afterwards I learned that it would be almost impossible for me to get pregnant. Distraught, and desperate for comfort, I'd told Zack.

I still remember what he said. "That's OK, babe, I wasn't planning on getting sprogged up for a few years yet anyway."

That told me what I needed to know. Not only hadn't it occurred to him the news might upset me, he hadn't even considered it from anyone's point of view but his own. He'd practically admitted he planned to use me and then dump me when my lack of fertility might not fit with his plans – and he'd fully expected me to go along with that. Thankfully, miserable though I was, I'd had just enough self respect to finish with him.

Mum must have been relieved at that, but she'd helped me through it without a word about her having told me so, or it being for the best. I was better off without him, but not for the reason she'd imagined.

"Mum, I know you thought he was a reckless driver, but he's never had an accident." I knew because I worked with his current wife. Seemed he was still insensitive, but he'd become a little more sensible.

"Well no, I wasn't happy about the speed he drove at but that's not why I didn't like him. He was making you unhappy; and at a time you needed support not more stress."

"You were right about him OK, just not about your premonition thing. I wouldn't have been killed in a car crash if I'd stayed with him."

"Is that what the premonitions are about?" Chrissie asked.

"They warn if someone will have an accident and die if they carry on with what they're doing?"

"Supposedly," I said just as Mum said, "No"

"No?" I asked.

"No. They just show that it's time for things to change."

"Oh they're going to change all right," Chrissie said. That nasty tone was back in her voice.

I ignored it and asked Mum about the incident that had started it all off. She'd told me lots of times about how, just after I'd been born, she'd been about to book into a hostel when she'd realised I'd lost a shoe. A baby shoe obviously. By the time she and my dad had gone back and found it the place had been fully booked. They'd gone to my grandma's instead hence avoiding whatever disaster had befallen those who'd booked in. I only then realised I didn't know what had happened and asked her to explain.

"It was something too horrific to tell the child I'd been when I first heard about it I suppose?"

"There was no disaster. Have I never told you?"

"No."

"We were trying to book into the hostel because we had nowhere else to go. Or thought we didn't. Your grandma hadn't liked me seeing so much of your dad; thought I was too young. I was still trying to talk her round when I realised I was pregnant. We cleared off rather than face up to her."

"But Grandma wasn't like that."

"She was a bit fierce back then. She mellowed a lot as she got older. But even then she wasn't as bad as I'd feared. I did get a bit of a telling off for being so silly but it was as much for avoiding telling her and taking off like we did as for getting pregnant. We neither of us had jobs and couldn't afford to marry, let alone set up home before you were born."

I nodded. I knew they weren't married until I was over a year old.

"After the lecture she had us come and live with her. We got married a year later and she hardly said anything about doing things the wrong way round. By the time you were a cute little schoolgirl and I was pregnant with your sister she'd decided things had worked out OK."

"So the shoe sort of got you and your mum back together?" Chrissie prompted.

"Yes. If we'd had somewhere else to go with the baby I'd not have turned up on her doorstep late one night."

"But it isn't always something like that? Getting people together? It was with Dad meeting Laura but it made her split up with someone before."

"As I said it's a sign of change, but I think the changes have always been for the best. And from what I hear another is due. You two haven't been getting on so well lately have you?"

If my face looked like Chrissie's she got that confirmed twice over.

"Why not? What's gone wrong?"

There was a long pause which I broke by saying, "Chrissie has seemed a bit cold and distant toward me."

"You started it!"

"I did not!"

"Did too, pushing me away, shutting me out."

"How have I, love?" I asked as gently as I could.

"Why didn't you tell me?" Tears ran down her face. "I tell

you stuff all the time. I thought you'd share it with me but you don't want me now, do you? I was OK before but not …" She continued talking but her sobs meant I couldn't make out any more.

I held her tight until she stopped crying, then found her a tissue.

"Chrissie love, I've no idea what you're talking about. If I had important news then of course I'd tell you. You're family."

She stared into my face as though trying to see beyond my words then turned to see Mum looking equally puzzled. "You don't know either?" she asked her.

Mum shook her head.

Chrissie turned back to me. "Oh my god! You don't know. You didn't tell me because you don't know! Or …it's not true. But… I was so sure." She squeezed my hand as though she thought I needed comfort.

"What is it, Chrissie? What don't we know?"

"I … I thought you were pregnant."

"You know that's not possible, love."

"Unlikely you said, not impossible. You've been feeling sick in the mornings."

"I have a couple of times but that's because there's a bug going round at work." I'm not usually susceptible to these things, but every new person that got it seemed to pass it on to me.

"And you've put on weight."

"Thanks!" I knew it was true. She was speaking with the honesty of someone close, not the distant and uninterested way she'd been treating me earlier.

"And you've been moody lately."

"Because I had a grumpy teenager to deal with," I pointed out. Although to be fair I wasn't entirely sure which of us had got that way first.

"And there's that," she pointed at my last delicious morsel of cake. Battenburg and until very recently I'd absolutely loathed marzipan.

Mum's mouth looked like it should have been on one of those big fish you sometimes see in dentist's waiting rooms, just hanging loose waiting for something to swim in. "When was your last time of the month?" she asked.

"Ages ago, but you know I've never been regular." I hadn't, which was part of my problem, but it had been months since the last time. "Could I be, do you think?" I was already thinking I could. I had felt different recently, truly I had.

Mum made me stand up and she felt my belly. She asked a few questions and said, "I think you should see your doctor."

"I will. I will."

Then I saw Chrissie's expression. She looked as miserable as I felt optimistic. She'd thought I'd kept the news from her, and I could see why that would upset her, but surely she could see that wasn't true. Did she think I'd reject her just as her mother had? I wouldn't. Having a child of my own was something I'd longed for, but it wouldn't make me truly happy if it meant losing the daughter I already had. Telling her wouldn't convince her though; I had to find a way to show her.

I reached out to her, with my hand and my heart. "Chrissie, I know it's a lot to ask but will you come to the doctor with me? I'll need someone with me… I'll be an emotional wreck; either way I expect. And I'd rather not say anything to your dad until I know."

"Don't you want Gran to go with you?"

I glanced at Mum. She gave me the tiniest of winks. I know she'd have been delighted to come with me and knew too why I wanted it to be Chrissie.

"I want you, Chrissie. If by some miracle I am pregnant the baby will be your brother or sister. I'll want both of my children to be close despite the age gap."

"No reason why they shouldn't be," Mum said. "Just look at you and your sister."

"You really want me? Not just at the doctor's I don't mean. You'll still want me even if you have a baby?"

"Of course I will, silly. Who else do you think will be my unpaid baby sitter?"

"That's more like it!" She was smiling though. "Hey if you are pregnant you're going to have to put up my pocket money."

"Oh?"

"How else am I going to afford to buy loads of cute stuff for my little bruv or sister?"

"I think you'll find that's what grandmothers are for," Mum said. "You call me the minute you know for sure and we'll go on a little shopping trip, Chrissie love."

"And buy cute baby shoes?"

"The cutest in the shop."

12. Tricks And Treats

"Look at this, isn't it cute?" Diane held up a jelly Dracula.

"No it's not and you're not seven. Put it back," her husband said.

"Yes, Dad," she said and stuck out her tongue.

"You're so childish," Mike complained.

"And you're no fun at all."

"Would you like any help with your packing?" asked the cashier.

"No thanks," they said together, exchanging tight smiles.

"Sorry, love," Mike said as he carried their bags to the car. "I don't mean to be so miserable. I'm fed up with all the hype and commercialism of, well, of just about everything. Hallowe'en, Christmas, Valentine's. The real meaning has been lost and replaced by marketing and a lot of cheap plastic rubbish."

"You have a point, especially about Christmas, but Hallowe'en can still be fun. I like seeing the kids come round all dressed up and stuff."

"They don't though, do they? One or two bung on a cheap plastic mask and then a gang of them demand money and sweets and threaten something nasty if you don't pay up. Demanding money with menaces, that's what it is."

"You're exaggerating. They're not all like that."

"No? Some of them appreciate the true meaning of it all do they? And what exactly is that anyway?"

"It's just a laugh, giving kids some happy memories. We used to have great Hallowe'en parties when I was a kid. Apple bobbing and home made toffee and scaring each other with ghost stories. It was fun."

"I suppose," he reached over and squeezed her hand.

Mike forgot their disagreement, until two days later; Hallowe'en. Searching through the wardrobe for the tie he thought would look best for a presentation at work, he found two costumes. The black dress, cape and pointed cap he guessed were for Diane. There was a sheet like arrangement that she was probably hoping to persuade him to wear.

The presentation went well, but all Mike could think about, as his boss congratulated him, was Diane. When he'd kissed her goodbye, she'd been wearing plastic fangs. If she'd done that last year, he'd have laughed, or teased her; something. This morning he'd only been interested in getting to work. She was right; lately he'd been no fun at all.

His boss was so happy about the presentation, he readily agreed to Mike finishing early. On the way home, he stopped at the supermarket for a few essentials.

"What on earth is going on here?" Diane asked when she returned from work.

"Sorry, I've made rather a mess."

"You have. What are you… are they toffee apples?"

"Oh no, my pretty, these are poisoned apples," Mike said in his best witch's voice.

Diane laughed and hugged him. "What about these?" She pointed to sticky pools of a white lumpy substance.

"Ghost vomit. Mostly melted marshmallows and syrup. I wouldn't eat them, if I were you."

"I won't. Nor those, I hope that's chocolate?" She pointed

out some brown dollops that looked as though they should be picked up with a pooper scooper.

"I haven't got a name for them; the kids will just have to use their imaginations."

"Kids?"

"Yeah, I've got a plan that'll guarantee every trick or treater in the area will be knocking on our door."

"Oh, Mike. I do love you."

"Just as well, because although your treat is that I'll wear that daft costume, I'm still playing some tricks. The first one is the disappearing husband."

"What?"

"Don't look so worried. I just meant I'm leaving you to clear up here and get our tea, whilst I sort out the lawn."

Mike wouldn't let Diane look until they'd eaten. He'd emptied a bag of compost into a rectangle and put a cross of plant supports at one end. It looked just like a freshly dug grave. He'd hung a cobweb like fishing net in the perfect position to brush against the face of anyone trying to ring the doorbell. The security light had been switched off, so everything was dimly illuminated by a string of icicle shaped Christmas lights.

"That'll do the trick, I think?" he asked.

"It's brilliant."

"He he, d'you hear what I said? Do the trick? Geddit?"

Diane shook her head. "I don't know what's come over you, but it's great to see you relaxed for a change."

"I was just thinking about what you said the other day. I'm not much fun lately. I've had a lot on my mind, but I've not been thinking about what's important." He stroked her bulging belly.

"You're worried about being a parent?"

"Not worried exactly. I was maybe overawed by the responsibility. I thought we'd have to be all sensible and grown up. That doesn't mean we can't have fun though. What sort of dad will I be if I can't have a laugh?"

"You do laugh and you'll be a great dad. Can we put the costumes on now?"

"Sure thing."

Mike did a silly ghost impression for each group of children. Diane then told their fortunes or cast spells on them as Mike distributed his handmade treats.

After a couple of hours all the sweets had gone.

"Phew, I'm shattered. It was fun though, wasn't it?" Diane asked.

"Yes, some of the kids were great, especially that vampire who got caught in the net."

"He was sweet, wasn't he? The zombies were good too. It must have taken ages to learn all those dance moves."

"Not to mention wrapping on the bandages."

"Those bigger kids with the masks weren't nice, pushing the little ones, snatching sweets without a word of thanks and throwing eggs on next door's car. I'd have liked to play a trick on them."

"Don't worry, we did. I made two batches of each kind of sweet. The nice kids got ones made with just chocolate and golden syrup. The thugs got ones with a few extra special ingredients."

Mike produced the empty packs for; prunes, frozen sprouts, anchovies and chilli powder.

13. Visiting As Santa

Jerry fidgeted on his nice comfortable cloud. It wasn't because of the far too warm red suit, or even the scratchy, snow-white false beard. It wasn't even the difficulty of mastering a jolly 'Ho Ho Ho' when he'd not spoken recently. He'd not spoken because he hadn't had a mouth, or any body at all. He'd almost got used to that and now, temporarily at least, he had one again.

Having a body, and it being short, fat and squishy rather than tall and lean as his original had been, was disconcerting, but not his biggest concern. Jerry was debating whether he should go down to Earth. If he did, would he be allowed back up? Nobody had talked about that other place and Jerry wasn't keen to learn about it from personal experience.

He'd been restless since shortly after his death. He'd been lucky in that there had been time for his wife to get to his side, tell him she loved him and kiss him goodbye. It had comforted him. Jerry hadn't been able to reply. That was frustrating at the time. Later he was glad.

"I'd just have reminded her about the life insurance policy," he admitted to the angel assigned to helping him settle in. "It would have been a waste. Everything's in order."

"What would have been better?" the angel asked.

"To tell her I love her and our son. Say sorry I would no longer be with them, not to grieve too long and wish them happiness if they can find it."

The angel had glowed at that. "It's not too late. Feel that wish now and it will reach them."

Jerry did try, quite a lot of the time. It was hard though. Hard to believe all this was true. Lively, brilliant, admired, successful Jerry Ballantyne dead. Gone. No longer important except as a memory to those he'd been closest to. It didn't seem possible. Also he couldn't help thinking about his funeral. Who would give the eulogy? Maybe there would be more than one as, young though he was, there was lots to say. Whoever wrote his obituary wouldn't struggle to come up with words of praise.

That Jerry was in heaven seemed right. Or almost right. He was still adjusting to the idea it was real, but didn't doubt his place there. He'd done well in life, building on the family business, making them all rich. Mum and Dad didn't say they were pleased or proud about that but he knew they must be. Their delight when he married Lisa and pride in their grandson had shown very clearly. He hoped they'd be of comfort to each other as they mourned him.

Jerry's angel had been very helpful in showing him around and explaining how everything worked. He didn't crowd Jerry, but somehow was always there when he had a question, or needed someone by his side.

"I'm glad you're here," Jerry said. "But surprised too. I wasn't exactly nobody, but would never have expected my own personal angel."

"Everyone gets one for as long as they need," the angel replied. "For those rejoining loved ones that's not long, but your family are still living."

"How do you mean everyone gets an angel?"

"Everyone, simple as that. For some the journey takes longer, but everyone with good in their soul eventually comes up here. When they arrive, one of us tries to help them settle."

"What if they're… ?" Jerry wasn't sure what he wanted to say. He knew religious beliefs didn't matter as he'd had none.

"Everyone," the angel repeated. Jerry understood; up here he was no better than anyone else. What an odd concept this whole heaven thing was proving to be.

He began to fret about how Lisa would cope without him. Jerry had looked after her, taken care of her. And their boy, Daniel; he'd be so lost without his father to guide him. These concerns seemed natural to Jerry. His angel didn't agree.

"You're dead now. Stop thinking and start feeling. That's the way to reach our loved ones."

"My family don't believe in life after death. They're not that…" He'd been going to say gullible. Lisa used to talk some soft headed notion of her gran looking down on her from heaven and smiling, to lift her spirits. Jerry had put her right. Except he hadn't actually been right, had he? It was all very confusing.

"Would you like to see your wife and child?" the angel asked.

"That's possible?"

"Usually we connect simply with our feelings, but that doesn't seem to be working for you." He gestured downwards.

"Lisa," he whispered as his wife came into view. She looked well, happy. "She's not grieving."

"You wished for her not to do so for long," the angel

reminded him.

"True but… Daniel!" There was no doubt the boy was his son, but he was no longer a baby just taking his first steps.

"A fine boy," the angel said.

"Yes, but he must be four years old and I've only been up here a few weeks."

"For some the journey here takes seconds, some years, some centuries."

"Oh. I don't remember the last few years," Jerry said.

"Forgetfulness is a blessing granted to the truly repentant."

"Ummm right. Hey! Who's that?" Jerry had seen the man but hadn't realised he was with his family. As Jerry watched, the man crouched down and whispered something to Daniel. The boy laughed and ran off in the direction the man had indicated.

Instead of rising to his feet, the man adjusted his position so one knee rested on the ground. He took hold of Lisa's hand and reached into his pocket for something which sparkled brightly.

Lisa first looked surprised and then delighted.

"No!" roared Jerry as he realised his wife was about to accept a proposal from another man.

Lisa's smile dissolved. Her lips moved and so did her free hand, meaning the man couldn't slip the ring onto her finger.

"She heard me?" Jerry asked.

"No. Felt you perhaps. As I said, feelings are the way to communicate."

"I don't want to see any more," Jerry told his angel.

The image vanished, but nothing else changed. Jerry still

felt the man's hope and Lisa's love.

"Isn't that what you wanted?" the angel asked. "Happiness for her and a good father for your son?"

"I thought so. I mean yes, of course I did but…"

"I'm sorry, I really thought this would help."

For all his insistence that feelings were the best method of communication, it seemed the angel hadn't really understand him at all. Just as well, because if the dark emotions of jealousy and resentment were obvious to all, Jerry might lose his nice comfortable cloud.

"Of course I want them to be happy," he'd said, trying to mean it. "But I don't know anything about that man. And he sent Daniel off. Why would he do that?"

"To draw a picture of Santa. They're going to visit soon."

"I never got to take him to see Santa."

"There is a way… but no, perhaps …"

"Tell me, please."

It took some persuading, but eventually the angel revealed that visitations to loved ones left behind were possible. Sometimes they were in dreams, songs or visions, sometimes a ghostly presence or a visit from Santa.

"I want to do that. Go back as Santa and see my boy."

"You have to be very sure. Anything you feel will be stronger there, will reach them so much more clearly. The same is true of their feelings."

"I'm sure." He could remind little Daniel of his real father, stop an imposter taking his place. Daniel would show his feelings for the man and Lisa would have to give him up.

"To go down, you have to leave here, Jerry."

"Obviously."

"You might not return quickly … or at all."

OK, maybe the angel did have an inkling of what was in Jerry's mind. Could he stop him going?

"I want to return to Earth as Santa and visit my son," Jerry thought with as much force as he could muster. He felt his body reform and an ill-fitting red suit cover it.

"I'll leave you to it then," the angel said.

Jerry fidgeted on his nice comfy cloud. After he'd gone down and done what he intended to do, would he sink lower still? Or perhaps he'd be permitted a slow journey back? Surely he would, because he was justified, wasn't he? He'd been hurt by what he saw. Angered. He'd do it and not be sorry. Unrepentant. Not blessed with forgetfulness.

Even so, he'd do it. He had Daniel to think about. Daniel and Lisa. They were important now, not him. Jerry would suffer for it, but he'd push that man away from them. Leave Lisa with no husband, Daniel with no father.

Jerry felt himself sink, then land. And then he felt so much more. The love he'd felt for Lisa as she walked down the aisle towards him. His joy when she told him she was pregnant. The overwhelming happiness he'd felt the first time he held Daniel.

"Ho ho ho!" he managed to croak out as his son ran towards him, arms outstretched.

Jerry felt Daniel's innocent enthusiasm, pleasure and hope. No need to ask if he'd been a good boy, the truth of that shone from him. Daniel clambered onto his lap and began to chatter about reindeer. No thoughts filled Jerry's head, instead emotion flooded his heart.

Jerry felt love surround him. From Daniel, from Lisa and from the man. Daniel's seemed to be directed at almost everyone and everything, as was right for a small boy in Santa's grotto. The stranger's wasn't just directed at Lisa, but also at Daniel. There was even a little for the man in the red suit, making the child smile. There was hope in him too. Hope Lisa would one day accept the ring he still carried.

Lisa loved her son. Loved him above else, but not to the exclusion of all others. She loved the man by her side, the man Jerry realised she'd told she needed time to think. She loved Jerry too. The real Jerry, not the dressed up version in front of her. She loved the Jerry who was just a memory.

Jerry remembered his plan to rip apart their happiness and replace it with renewed grief and loss. He concentrated on radiating his feelings. He thought he heard a tearing sound. Was it working?

The man trembled as though hit by a strong invisible current. A quiet but unmistakeable metallic clang caused Lisa to look down. Jerry had made a hole in the man's pocket so the ring could fall through.

The man stooped to retrieve it and moved his hand towards another, intact, pocket.

'There's a safer place for that,' Jerry thought. 'A better place.' He concentrated on really feeling the words and his intent.

Lisa held out her hand and the man slipped the ring onto her finger.

"Merry Christmas," Jerry said. "And congratulations."

Lisa gave him the smile he remembered. "Thanks, Santa."

Jerry tried to give a final, "Ho ho ho!" but felt himself rise and was back on his nice comfy cloud before he'd finished.

14. My Cottage Isn't Haunted

I've always been a down to earth sort of girl. I don't believe in fate, fairytales or haunted houses. Coincidences and surprises happen, I'll admit that. And atmosphere is real. My little cottage has the good kind.

When I say cottage, I really mean a mid-terrace, two up, two down. Small, but cosy and I liked it the moment the estate agent ushered me in. I felt it was somewhere I could be happy. If it wasn't so fanciful, I'd say the house wanted me to be happy.

I don't believe in love at first sight, shared destiny or any similar romantic notions either. Physical attraction, that's all it is really.

"Soulmates," that's what Ryan said we were.

We got on well and had a few things in common, I'll grant you. The same taste in music, both way too fond of pizza, and OK at sixteen I did think I was in love. But it didn't really mean anything. Like I said, I'm the practical sort. Not the kind to marry her childhood sweetheart. Thought I could do better than a lad working in a hardware shop, hoping for an apprenticeship.

When I met Jack, a businessman, it seemed I had done better. He didn't make me laugh as Ryan had, nor talk to me much, but he was handsome and charming. For a while I did believe in that true love stuff. Jack was my one and only.

Poor man had no luck. His investments lost money. Friends cheated him. Nothing worked out for him.

"Except for you," he said. "You're everything to me."

Even I couldn't keep him out of prison.

"I was at work then, it wasn't me," he said to explain why he'd ignored the speeding ticket, not attended court.

I didn't understand any of it, but there was a photo of our car sure enough. I gave him the money and that should have been the end of it, but somehow he was summonsed for contempt. Madness!

He begged me not to go to the trial. "I don't want you to hear those lies."

Lies was right. He got five months.

For a while I was angry. With him, the lawyers, the judge. He assured me he would prove his innocence. Sort it out. In the meantime I lost the big house and bought my cottage. I was coping by the time Jack came out. No; more than that. I felt in control of my life. Settled in my new home.

Jack didn't take to it as I had. The cottage didn't like him. His words. The kettle cut off before it boiled so his tea was lukewarm. The lights failed and he stubbed his toe. As for the plumbing…

"It's haunted!" he claimed. The water went cold when he was in the shower. Sink overflowed when he tried to shave. "It makes terrible noises. They keep me awake when you work nights." It left him too tired to apply for jobs.

I found him one on a building site.

"Labouring?" his tone told me it was beneath him.

"Until you find another way to pay for the steaks you eat, wine you drink and suits you wear."

I was tired and fed up. Plumbing can't be haunted, so he was making excuses. Or lying to me. Once that thought entered my head, it wouldn't leave. It felt as though it should always have been there, as indeed it should.

I did some research. Discovered his court case hadn't been for non-payment of a speeding ticket, but fraud. He had been involved in dodgy investment schemes, but not in the way he'd said. He'd lied about everything. He wasn't the victim – I was. One of many.

There seemed little point in doing anything more than kick him out. Chalk it up to experience. Not to luck or the fate I've never believed in any more than I have ghosts in the pipework. When the water refused to heat for my shower it wasn't the spirit world turning against me, simply the ancient boiler breaking down. I called a plumber to install a new one.

The plumber was Ryan. I suppose some would say that was fate, bringing him back into my life. Or maybe my haunted cottage had found a way to reunite me with my soulmate? Nah, that's just the way things work out sometimes. We've been back together for a while now, me and Ryan in our little cottage. Do you know what? There finally is something I'm starting to believe in; that we'll live happily ever after.

15. Gold Star Baby Seat

The doorway to Andrea's office was blocked by someone backing out.

"What on earth are you doing with my chair?"Andrea asked.

Karen shrugged. "I just wanted to try it."

"Why? They're all the same."

"They're not. I don't believe that." Karen looked like she might cry.

"Come on, it's OK. I'm not angry and I can see you've brought up a replacement." Andrea put her arm around her employee. "I was just worried you'd hurt yourself. Now tell me what this is about."

Karen tipped up the chair she'd been in the process of removing, to reveal the large gold star stuck underneath. "I've been trying to get pregnant for over a year. You don't need it now, do you?"

"Not that one, no." She hadn't been aware she'd had it at all and tried not to wonder how long it had been behind her desk. Divorced and just turned forty, a baby would be quite a risk even without Andrea's history.

She asked Grant to help carry the chair down for Karen. The girl looked so happy Andrea could almost believe it would work. The gold star chair's reputation was just a silly rumour of course. Although several people who'd used it had gone on to have babies, that was hardly surprising. The company, started by Andrea's grandparents, employed mainly young women.

Originally the bulk of the work was typing. With everyone having computers now Andrea had needed to diversify. They did some proofreading work and a little translation, but mostly she provided temporary administration staff to other companies. Presumably, on occasion, because their own pregnancy chair had struck lucky!

The first 'victim' of the gold star chair was replaced for her maternity leave by someone already pregnant who wanted a few month's work before her baby was due.

"Can't really count that, can you?" Andrea had argued when the rumours started. "And a lot of people have sat in it without becoming pregnant."

Some girls deliberately sat in that particular seat. Some went to lengths to avoid it. Some claimed not to want anything to do with it, but Andrea had seen them sit in it when they arrived early or when they thought everyone else had gone home. Andrea had never knowingly sat in it herself.

She hadn't wanted to chance it. She'd been pregnant once, long before the chair arrived. After she lost the baby, and was told the chances of another late miscarriage were high, she hadn't wanted to try again. She couldn't bear to repeat such heartbreak. Not even if the risk might mean a baby, might mean staying married.

Perhaps she'd been wrong. She'd never forget the child she'd lost. Never not hurt when she thought of him, but the pain had lessened over the years. It became a sadness kept to the back of her mind most of the time. The pain of being childless though, that grew stronger every day. The loneliness of her life wasn't quite obliterated by work.

The chair hadn't worked its magic for nearly a year. Perhaps it had been in Andrea's office all that time? A man had applied for the latest, due to maternity leave, vacancy. Very few men applied and when they did Andrea was reluctant to employ them. In a mainly female office that could be a distraction. Equality laws meant she couldn't refuse to consider anyone based on gender though, so there had been exceptions. Some had caused as much disruption as she'd feared. A couple of men had been very good employees whom she'd been sorry to lose when they moved on. One was still employed for occasional translation, but worked almost exclusively from home.

When she'd interviewed Grant, Andrea found that rather than discouraging him by stressing the lack of opportunities, she said, "Although this particular job is part time, there may be other similar roles on a full time basis which the successful candidate could be transferred into."

"Part time is fine to start with," he told her.

Grant, who was single, had a good reason for wanting such a job; his four-year-old daughter Lulu. The hours would fit well around school.

"I've mostly been a stay at home dad, just doing some bar work in the evenings while Lulu stayed with her grandparents."

He'd done some admin before that and recently taken part in a 'back to work' scheme so his skills were current. Grant wasn't as young as most of her other staff, two years older than Andrea in fact. He wasn't distractingly good looking either. A bit of grey in his hair. A few wrinkles. Or maybe they were laughter lines? He seemed cheerful and pleasant.

As she'd showed him around the main office and invited him to demonstrate his ability to operate a computer and photocopier no one paid Grant any more attention than if he'd been a female applicant. He shouldn't be a disruption at all, Andrea decided. In fact having someone older and steadier on the staff could be an advantage.

She was half right. Grant was a valuable employee and excellent at smoothing over minor disagreements amongst the girls. For some reason though she found herself spending increasingly frequent periods of time in the main office rather than her own on the floor above. It certainly wasn't because her chair was uncomfortable. As she'd told Karen they were all exactly the same.

It meant nothing that she'd recently been using the gold star version. Even so perhaps she shouldn't have been surprised the rumours had started up again the moment she and Grant announced they were to get married and Andrea was to become Lulu's stepmother.

16. A Swirl Of Tea

It took Florence some time to locate the glass tea pot they'd been given as a wedding present. Not surprising perhaps as their next anniversary would be their tenth and they'd moved house four years ago. The pot was a lovely shape, almost a work of art and Florence had been pleased to be given it, but after the initial novelty of using it had worn off they'd taken to just dropping teabags into mugs if they wanted tea. That wasn't often as both she and Robin preferred coffee.

Aunt Dorothy, that's who'd given it to them. A great believer in the power of a nice cup of tea was Aunt Dorothy. "There are times when nothing else will quite do," she'd told Florence and Robin as though sharing a lifetime of wisdom.

Now Florence watched the tea gradually colour the water. The leaves swirled a little and blossomed out making Florence think of the birds they'd seen silhouetted against gorgeous sunsets on honeymoon. It was relaxing to watch the process of the tea brewing. It wouldn't take long; not enough time for her to feel she should be doing anything more useful than watching. Just long enough for the tea to reach the perfect temperature to drink. It was a pleasing equation that. Too weak and it would also be too hot. Too strong and it would be too cool, but get one thing just right and the other would be too.

Florence tipped biscuits onto a plate, poured milk into her cup and then added the tea. She took a sip. Ah, that was better. Aunt Dorothy had been right.

It had been an unsettling kind of day. No major disasters or anything like that, but Florence had been... well, unsettled despite what should have been a good start. She had got up in plenty of time to share breakfast with her husband. They didn't often manage that so when they did, Florence liked to make proper coffee and a teeny bit of a fuss about it. She'd scrambled four eggs and buttered toast, then given it all to Robin.

"I know they say to feed a cold," he said. "But mine's almost gone."

"Don't eat it all if you don't want it. I just couldn't face it."

"I hope you're not going down with anything?"

"No, I feel fine." She did. Fine but restless somehow.

The coffee had tasted bitter.

"Sorry, I must have had the water too hot," she said.

"Tastes fine to me."

She should have worked out what was behind it all by then. Certainly her mother, grandmother or Aunt Dorothy would have done had she called them and told them about just those few minutes.

At work she'd done all that was required of her but couldn't shake the feeling that there was something she should have done, or which she'd forgotten about. The coffee there had tasted bitter too, but that was easily explained. They were supplied with whichever brand of instant was on special offer and currently that wasn't any of the better ones.

She'd been hungry at lunchtime, thanks to skipping breakfast and bought the larger sized layered salad and a bottle of mineral water. She'd enjoyed the colourful leaves, crunchy carrots, spicy radish and all the rest, but somehow it hadn't been satisfying.

Florence had stopped at the supermarket on the way home. Her purchases included biscuits. Nothing low fat or high fibre, but gorgeously crumbly puff pastry filled with rich, sweet lemon cream.

She bit into one, sending a shower of delicate crumbs onto her work blouse. Fabulous. Florence finished her tea and poured another cup. She resisted finishing off the biscuits; she'd save them to share with Robin.

"Come and sit down," she said when he came in. "I've got a surprise for you."

He certainly looked surprised when she placed the teapot before him. "Tea?"

"Yes. And biscuits but that's not the surprise. Do you remember Aunt Dorothy saying there was a time when nothing else would do?"

"Hmmm, funny old bird."

"She was right though." Florence produced a small plastic wand and drew his attention to the thin blue line. "Mum went off coffee too when she was expecting me."

Robin picked her up and swung her round, just as though she were a tea leaf in the pot and she felt his love pour out and fill the room.

17. Always There

"Mummy, Freddie will always be my friend, won't he?" Simon asked.

How was she supposed to answer? Caroline knew what her son needed to hear, but also knew it wasn't true.

Caroline distracted Simon with a pot of yoghurt and got him ready for school. He'd ask again though and she'd have to answer.

That answer would have to be, 'No.' Caroline should know. Hadn't her own mother once promised she'd be with her always?

The first suggestion this wasn't true came when Caroline became pregnant. Mum had been ecstatic and hugged her, gabbling plans for shopping and decorating the nursery. It was only then Caroline realised how quiet and listless Mum had been over the last few months.

"Mum, is everything OK?"

"I've not been too well lately, but it's probably nothing."

The nothing turned out to be cancer, but still Mum insisted Caroline and her husband, Paul, weren't to worry about her.

"I've seen my beautiful girl grow into a lovely young woman and marry a wonderful man and I know my family will continue." She laid her hand on Caroline's swelling belly. "One life is ending, but another's starting. That's the one you should concern yourself about."

"Mum, don't say that! You said you'd always be there for

me, always love me."

Mum had put her arm around Caroline "I will always love you, wherever I am."

Paul converted his home office into a bedroom for Mum. "I can work just as easily in the dining room," he assured them.

The chemo made Mum feel sick, but she didn't complain. Instead she cut out spicy foods, swapped acidic fruits for bananas and said, "Don't worry."

Either the chemo or Caroline's pregnancy acted as a tonic on Mum. She was in remission for Simon's premature birth.

"Will he be OK?" Caroline asked as she cradled her tiny son.

"Of course, love. You're here for him, giving him strength," Mum assured her.

Mum's cancer wasn't mentioned at Simon's first birthday party, or his second. By the time he started school, his premature birth was almost forgotten.

"I told you he'd be fine," Mum said as they watched him playing in his sand pit. She wouldn't talk about her own deteriorating medical condition other than, "Don't worry about me."

"I can't help it, Mum."

"Simon's calling you, love."

Simon had made a sand something and was calling for her to admire it. Caroline marvelled at his creation and at her own. Her son was almost as tall as other boys his age now. The sun had bleached his hair and darkened his freckles from the hours he spent playing outside. Simon never seemed to get tired.

As the young family needed her less and Simon got

stronger, Mum faded away. She died quietly giving them time to say goodbye.

Paul was wonderful. He arranged the funeral, cared for Simon and held Caroline while she cried and cried. "I'll always be here for you," he said. "I'll always love you."

By then, Caroline knew they were promises he couldn't guarantee to keep, even if he wanted too. She wanted to comfort Simon, who missed his granny, but how could she? To promise he always had her would be a lie.

His mother's distress unsettled Simon. He stopped talking, hardly ate. He tired easily and it was hard to get him interested in anything. Then Freddie put in an appearance.

Caroline was going through the motions of shopping, not really caring what went in the trolley, when Simon picked up a jar of apricot jam. Apricot was Mum's favourite preserve, but she could only manage liquid food towards the end, so they'd not had any in the house for some time. Jam might not be particularly nutritious, but anything which tempted Simon to eat had to be a good thing.

Simon ate three pieces of bread and jam followed by a banana when they got back from shopping. That simple meal was about all he would eat, but at least he was happy to have it every day.

The following week, Simon picked up a tin of salmon. "Can we have this, Mummy?"

She happily took the tin from him. She was so pleased to hear his voice, she'd have agreed to anything.

"Yes, love. I didn't know you liked fish?"

"Freddie says I will."

Simon mentioned Freddie frequently over the next few days. He thought Simon should eat more, play outside and brush his teeth. Caroline was happy except for Simon seeking reassurance they'd always be friends.

"Who is Freddie?" Her mother's name had been Frederica, but Caroline couldn't think of anyone actually called Freddie. "Is he a new boy at school?"

"No, Mummy. He's too big for school."

Rather than scare Simon with her fears, Caroline stayed calm and spoke to Paul when he came home from work.

"Maybe he's perfectly harmless, but I don't like the idea of a stranger talking to our son."

"We'll find out as much as we can tonight, then we'll speak to the headmistress tomorrow," Paul said.

At tea that evening, Paul said, "I hear you've got a new friend, Simon?"

Simon nodded.

"He's called Freddie, isn't he?" Paul prompted.

Simon nodded again.

"I thought we might go out somewhere on Saturday, perhaps Freddie might like to come?"

Caroline dropped her fork and gasped, but Paul gave her a reassuring nod.

Simon looked thoughtful. "He'd like to go to the zoo," he said eventually.

"Shall we ask him then?" Paul asked.

"I just did, Daddy."

"Oh, is he here?"

"Yes, but you can't see him."

Caroline breathed a sigh of relief. Am imaginary friend was so much better than a real... She didn't want to consider the possibilities.

The visit to the zoo was a success. Simon ate all the lunch they bought for him and chattered the whole time. Freddie wasn't mentioned until the journey home and even then, Simon just reported Freddie had enjoyed the trip. Simon's appetite and conversation were fully restored after that and his teacher reported he was doing much better at school.

"Does he mention Freddie?" Caroline asked.

"Occasionally," the teacher admitted, "but please don't worry about that. Having an imaginary friend is very common."

Freddie was good for Simon. He told him not to be scared of the dentist and helped him with tying his laces. He reminded Simon to say please and thank you. Freddie was an excellent friend and one who could stay with Simon forever, if that's what he wanted.

Caroline almost laughed out loud as that thought occurred to her. Next time Simon asked about Freddie, she could give him the answer he wanted.

Freddie came on lots of family outings but his favourite was always the zoo. He loved to see the giraffes.

Simon said, "They tickle his hand, when he strokes their noses."

Caroline didn't ask how Freddie knew that. It had been years since the zoo allowed people to get close enough for the giraffes to reach down their long necks and sniff the hands of giggling children. Freddie was right though, it did tickle. Caroline remembered from when Mum used to take her.

"What are you thinking about?" Paul asked.

"Mum."

"You were smiling."

"Yes. I remembered how she used to take me to the zoo."

"We'll go again this weekend then," Paul said.

"Simon, what does Freddie look like?" Caroline asked as they watched the penguins being fed.

"Oh, you know." He shrugged.

"No, I can't see him, remember?"

Simon described Freddie's red-gold hair, his funny hat, bright green scarf and matching gloves. Caroline had been wrong, she could see Freddie, except her version wasn't a little boy. As Simon continued to talk, Caroline saw a memory of her mother. Mum, wearing her new scarf and gloves, had taken her to the zoo. They'd had a picnic, the sandwiches filled with a choice of salmon or apricot jam all washed down with a flask of hot chocolate.

"Come on, let's get ice creams for you boys and drinks for the grown ups. Hot chocolate for me and Daddy, vanilla with a flake for you and raspberry ripple for Freddie; that's his favourite."

"That's right, Mummy."

Did it matter that Freddie only existed in Simon's mind? Not really. Did it matter that Mum now only existed in memories and Caroline's heart? Not really, because she'd always be there. She'd always love Caroline, just as she and Paul would always be there for each other and always love Simon.

18. Dreaming Of Seventh Heaven

Donna often had weird dreams. Whilst asleep they always seemed to make sense however odd they were. Once she woke, she'd wonder if there was some deep meaning to them, if only she could interpret them properly. The stranger they were, the more she thought they must mean something.

She didn't have to think too hard about the dream with the gypsy. The woman wasn't dressed in shawls and hoop earrings, nor was she called Rose-Lee, or Magical Madge. Donna and the gypsy weren't in a tent, or Romany caravan; they were in a boat. The woman didn't have a crystal ball, the small room they were in didn't rock and she couldn't see out, but the sleeping Donna had known she was with a gypsy, in a boat, travelling North.

The gypsy said that true love would come Donna's way. There wasn't any mention of tall, dark and handsome, but he'd have, "A heart beating strong and to him she'd belong."

Donna would know when she had the right man, because of something to do with the number seven.

"Go with lucky seven, you'll always be in heaven," the gypsy said.

Well, it was something like that. It was difficult for her to remember as she'd been asleep. It was all in rhymes, she did remember that. Of course, Donna immediately decided the gypsy had been referring to Stephen. He said Donna was his girl and she knew she made his heart beat faster, so it almost had to be. To be honest, Donna didn't pay too much attention after the bit where she was told what she wanted to know. Yes, even in dreams we only hear what we want to.

There was a warning too; there's always a warning isn't there? Near as she could remember it was, "From all the sevens stay away, something, something, will surely part. Dumbedy dumbedy day, then he'll break your heart." She missed most of it because she was dreaming about Stephen. Day dreaming whilst in a dream; how weird was that? Still, she was in love – or thought so anyway.

In the morning, she remembered the bit about seven and heaven. Donna decided that she must have misheard the warning and it was eleven she had to stay away from. The gypsy must have meant Dave, she reasoned. He lived at number eleven and a while back she'd been out with him a couple of times.

Stephen; that even sounded a bit like seven and there's seven letters in it and he lived at number seven and Donna met him in Seventh Heaven nightclub and he was gorgeous!

He proposed the day after her dream; at seven minutes past seven in the evening. He suggested they marry quickly; on the seventh of July. She'd only have known him seven weeks by then. In normal circumstances, she'd have worried about that but, because of the dream, she just took it as a sign. Talking of signing, she transferred all seven thousand pounds of her savings over to him. Why not? They'd soon be married and they needed it as a deposit for a house. She hoped they'd live at number seven and have seven children and…

A week before the wedding, she discovered the truth. Stephen, or whatever his name really was, had gone. So had her money, of course. It was no consolation that she wasn't the only one who'd been cheated. He had other, 'fiancées'.

You've guessed it, six more fools had been taken in.

That all happened almost a year ago. She was devastated, as you can imagine. Dave was very kind. Much kinder than she deserved after she'd heartlessly dumped him for her 'lucky' seven man. By then, even an idiot like Donna had sussed out that the warning to avoid all the sevens was supposed to make her see sense over Stephen. Maybe it was her subconscious warning her? Not once did Dave point out he knew how it felt to have a broken heart. He never told her she'd been stupid. He offered a shoulder to cry on.

Eventually, she realised for herself how stupid she'd been. Not over Stephen; that guy was a practised con artist and she didn't stand a chance. It was Dave she'd been stupid about. Why hadn't she seen what a wonderful man he was?

Donna had the dream again. The gypsy repeated her warning; all the sevens would break her heart. That's what she'd said (or her subconscious had said) and she (or it) was right. Maybe the first part of the dream would come true too? All she needed was the one seven to prove that Dave and she would be in heaven forever.

Donna couldn't find one. His birthday wasn't the seventh, he wasn't a seventh child, he wasn't born under the seventh sign of the zodiac. The nearest she got was that he lived at number eleven, if she added the two ones together and added it to her birthday, the fifth, that came to seven. She knew that wasn't the sign. Donna also knew she loved Dave. When he proposed, she accepted. Donna thought she could work in a seven somewhere.

She was wrong about that. They got married on the twelfth, had two bridesmaids, three tiers on the cake. Dave asked her to book ten days leave for the honeymoon.

The honeymoon was the sign. They travelled north to

begin a boating trip. Donna recognised the cabin as the place from her dream where the gypsy had spoken to her. The gypsy had been right: Donna did feel as though they were in heaven as they sailed gently along the river Severn.

19. Tina's Transformation

"The gorgeous new guy I was telling you about is coming along the corridor now," Becky said from her vantage point by the photocopier.

Tina rushed over to look through the office doorway. She blinked as the tall, blond young man walked passed; could it really be who she thought it was?

"Hey, stop drooling. I saw him first," Becky joked.

Realising she'd been staring, Tina returned to her desk. "I wasn't drooling."

"No, actually you look more like you've seen a ghost. What's up?"

"Nothing. I thought for a minute that I knew him."

"Knew, but didn't like, by the look on your face. What did he do?"

"Ruined my life," Tina said.

"God, really?"

"Well, maybe not, but it felt like it at the time. I was only fifteen."

"He didn't get you pregnant?"

Tina laughed. "No, nothing as terrible as that. Besides, that was ten years ago. Even if it is the same guy, we've both grown up and moved on since then."

The girls carried on with their work. Tina typed as efficiently as ever, but her mind wasn't on the job. She had changed in the last ten years, she assured herself. She was no longer the plump, nervous girl at the school disco with braces, cheap glasses and frizzy hair. She wasn't wearing the flouncey pink dress she'd worn when she was her sister's bridesmaid and which had become too tight. Tina had become a confident career woman, in a smart tailored suit. She forced herself to smile and showed off straight, white teeth. Her hair was in a neat French pleat. The girls who surrounded her now were friendly colleagues, not other schoolgirls teasing her and daring her to ask someone to dance.

Remembering the sick dread in her stomach as she'd crossed the dance floor, Tina shuddered. She'd intended to just walk away from the girls who'd teased her and try to keep out of their way until her dad came to collect her. Without realising it, she'd headed straight for Dean Cassidy. He'd seen her approaching and smiled. She was so close, it would have seemed weird not to say something. She didn't want Dean to think she was weird; he was so good looking and had the most wonderful blue eyes and the kind of blond hair she secretly longed to run her fingers through.

"Will you dance with me?" she'd blurted out.

"Sure," he'd replied and glanced over his shoulder to his mates. "If you wear a bag on your head."

He'd roared with laughter, as had his friends. As she ran out of the hall, it seemed everyone else was laughing at her too. She'd shut herself in the toilets until it was time to go home.

Study leave had started soon after, so by faking illness for a few days, she'd only had to go in to school for her exams and therefore avoided listening to the jokes she knew would be circulating about her. On several occasions she'd cried herself to sleep. Tina changed from shy to sullen and reclusive. Her exam results had been good though. She'd had nothing but revision to concentrate on, anything else was too painful to think about.

"Sorry to interrupt you, Tina." Her boss's voice brought her back to the present.

"I'd like to introduce you to the new marketing genius; Dean Cassidy."

Tina looked up into a pair of the most wonderful blue eyes. No doubt about it, he was the same person.

"Dean, this is Christina Jones, your opposite number here in the despatch department."

"Pleased to meet you," Dean said and offered his hand.

She was sure he didn't recognise her. That wasn't surprising, even if he did recall the incident that had devastated her, he'd remember an ugly kid called Chrissie.

Tina found herself an outsider again. Everyone else seemed taken in by Dean's easy charm and good looks. The men envied him and the girls apparently all fancied him. She resented the way he could talk confidently to anyone he met. It was clear he'd never known what it felt like to be humiliated. Every time she saw him, Tina was reminded of the unattractive, nervous kid who was still a part of her.

Each time Dean greeted her pleasantly, fetched her a coffee, agreed to one of her business suggestions, she remembered the first words he'd ever spoken to her. Would it really have been so hard for him to have been polite to her then? A simple 'no thanks', would still have hurt a little, but wouldn't have caused the complete humiliation she'd faced. If he'd troubled himself to be pleasant, she'd have been ecstatic instead of miserable. He might have been embarrassed then though, instead of enjoying a cheap laugh at her expense. He should be embarrassed. He should learn what that felt like.

"I'll see you at the dance, I hope?" he asked after a management meeting.

Tina shook her head. She'd let herself get obsessed about the school disco and was now imagining things.

Dean looked disappointed. "I was sure you were going. Didn't I hear you talking about your costume?"

Of course, he meant the Hallowe'en fancy dress ball the company was holding. Tina had joked with Becky that she'd dress as the witch they all thought she was. She'd laughed then, knowing none of them considered her witch-like either in behaviour or appearance. This was going to be one dance where Tina most definitely didn't get humiliated.

"Oh, yes, I'm going. I'll see you there." Hallowe'en was the perfect time for Tina to eradicate the painful ghosts of her youth. "I'm looking forward to it very much."

The day of the dance, Tina added the finishing touch to her costume. It was a hood made from a large, black cloth bag. When she put on the outfit, she smiled at her reflection. The costume showed of her figure rather well and the shadows created by the hood lent her a mystical, almost exotic beauty. Striding into the hall, she knew that people were looking at her. As they'd done ten years ago, people remarked on her clothes, her metal-work and her eyes. But no one asked if she'd stolen her dress from a little fat fairy. No one called her four eyes. Instead they admired her outfit and the bat and moon shaped jewellery. They said the way she'd made-up her eyes gave her gaze a hypnotic quality.

Tina circulated, laughing, drinking blood coloured cocktails and chatting. She was enjoying herself eating eye of newt quiche and listening to the band. Across the room, she saw Dean. Someone told her there had been a mix-up at the hire shop and instead of a Dracula suit, he'd been sent a groom's tuxedo. He'd been telling people he'd come as the condemned man. Tina felt her lips curl; how appropriate.

Dean returned her smile and crossed the dance floor towards her.

"Tina, will you dance with me?"

This was her chance. The moment she'd fantasised about, on and off, for almost ten years. She'd show Dean Cassidy she was as good as him. No, that she was better than him.

"Sure, Dean." She glanced behind her at Becky and the other girls from her department. "If you'll wear… this." Tina tucked a sprig of ivy into his button hole.

He frowned.

"It's OK, it's not really poison ivy; that sign was just put up to keep the junior staff away from the photocopier."

"What?"

"I've heard of people getting carried away at office parties and photocopying things they shouldn't. So I draped the machine in ivy and put up a sign saying it was poison ivy and would give a nasty rash to anyone who touched it. It's perfectly safe really though, I promise."

"It's not that, I thought you were going to say… Well, you reminded me of something awful I did years ago."

He remembered?

"What happened, Dean?"

"I was at a school dance. The other boys teased me because I was so tall and had stupid floppy blond hair."

"It's not nice to be teased."

"No, but that's no excuse for what I did."

"Go on."

"There was this girl, kind of cute with curly hair. She asked me to dance. I knew she was shy and it must have been really difficult for her to ask, but instead of being nice, I said something awful. The poor kid rushed out crying and I never saw her again. Whenever I see anyone shy, I think of her and feel bad."

"It's been ten years; you've both grown up and moved on since then."

"I suppose. I'd do anything to know I was forgiven."

"Even wear a bag over your head?" Tina pulled off her hood, revealing her curly hair. She handed the hood to Dean.

"So, it is you… Chrissie?"

Tina nodded.

"You remembered me, what I said?"

"Yes, but I think it's time we both forgot about it, don't you?" She didn't wait for his reply, instead she took his hand. "Come on, I've waited ten years to dance with you, don't keep me waiting any longer."

20. Battle Of The Parking Space

*Conflict noun **Kon**-flikt*

"A personality clash, Mandy," my boss said.

He's not interested; brushing it under the carpet as a childish squabble. So it is. Tasha is childish and I won't tolerate her petty jibes. I was allocated that parking space by George last week. She shouldn't put her car there. I'm going to use it even if I have to leave home earlier in the mornings. It's the best space – on its own so no idiot can knock their doors into my paintwork and it's sheltered by the wall of the maintenance department. On wet, windy days it's the only place that allows me to reach my desk without looking like I've lost a battle with the elements.

"Thanks, George," I say to the maintenance man, when he tells me the gate combination will change on Monday. Can't complain, it's the first change we've had this year.

"I'll tell Tasha," I offer. It's so sweet of him to come and tell me personally when he could have just emailed.

Oh, he has emailed everyone. Tasha must have been included, so I won't bother her with something she already knows.

Man against man, man against himself, man against the elements.

Ha! Beat her to it. Her car isn't here. I'll tangle the chain on the gate to make sure I have time to park and get inside before she can have a go at me. I had enough aggro from the kids this morning, for waking them early and making them rush.

As if I haven't enough to put up with, I get some weirdo heavy breathing at me. I bet Tasha knew it was a pervert when she put the call through. I'm sure I heard her laughing.

"I can see you're busy; I'll make the coffee," she says.

Well, that's big of her. Maybe she did mean to be nice, but I'd have been more convinced about that if she hadn't spilled some of mine.

1. a serious disagreement.

The bitch! She's still carrying on as though I'm the one in the wrong. It's my turn to make coffee. I don't rush. Hopefully she'll get a call from the pervert while I'm in the kitchen. He can tell her he's got something she wants – he might have for all I know.

Tasha's got something I want; a decent stapler. If she's going to accuse me of behaving badly, I might as well do it.

Better wait until she's out the room before I ask the boss if I can go early tonight. What's it to Tasha what time I go? She hates kids anyway, so I'm damn sure she'd rather be in the office typing than taking my two to the dentist. Come to think of it, so would I.

I stop at a phone box and give her another call. It hurts my throat wheezing like that, but it's worth it to let her share what I'm going through.

2. a long standing armed struggle.

Bugger it. My kids hate me because early mornings mean early nights and missed TV. They hate me because I've got to take them back to the dentist – as though I'll be getting some kind of pleasure from watching their terror as the needle and drill approach. And to cap it all, that bitch has been petty enough to come in even earlier and take my space!

Listening to the news at lunchtime puts things into perspective. So many innocent lives lost. And less innocent; people who were fighting for what they believed. Right or wrong – who knows? Compared to that, a bit of friction in the office is nothing.

When the pervert calls, I tell him what a coward he is. For once, he's the one to hang up.

3. *a difference of opinions, principles, etc*

Here was I ready to forgive and forget and she's been messing up the stuff around my computer. I had two pictures of the kids, an unidentifiable papier-mâche thing Chloe made and three hideous dolls old George in maintenance brought me back from his holidays. Tasha used to be his blue-eyed girl and the look on her face when she saw she'd been upstaged made me thank him sweetly for the first one and lean it against the photo frame.

This isn't the first time they've been knocked over… Hell, it's the first time I'm sure anything's gone missing. I've only got one picture of the kids now, but I thought one must have got blown away that time the window broke. Stuff got knocked on the floor by the maintenance team and they crawled around on the floor picking everything up. I can't remember if I've seen it since then. There are now only two of the horrible dolls. I suppose this is someone's idea of a joke?

"You're so rarely at your desk, Mandy, I'm surprised you can remember what was there," Tasha the bitch bitched.

I've a good mind to collect traffic cones and block all the spare spaces so she's got nowhere to park and never makes it to hers. Bitch said it was slander to accuse her of theft. I didn't even do that – just said I wanted the photo back. It must have been her. Who else would do it?

The phone rings. It's the perv. I ring maintenance right away, but they tell me there's no way to trace it and offer to change my extension number again.

Who is doing it?

*verb khun-**flikt***

It's not funny now. The last picture of the kids has gone. Losing the whatever it was that Chloe made wasn't funny either. Nor was it when the dolls went, one by one. I reported that when I realised it was more than just a silly joke. I didn't like them, in fact I've long since regretted putting them on the computer – but couldn't sling them without upsetting George.

I even took one to the stationery office when I worked there for a week because I knew he'd see it. Damn…

…took it and left it there and forgot. I'd apologise to Tasha if it wasn't for the fact I'm damn sure she's taken the others. And the picture of the kids. We lost the original when the computer crashed so I can't get another. Besides, you don't mess with somebody's kids.

I'm almost sure it's her. It has to be someone who's in early.

(of opinions, stories, etc.) disagree or be different.

Bill says that if I get the kids up any earlier it's not going to be worth them going to bed. He has a point, poor loves do seem tired and Tom has stopped asking to stay up and watch cop shows. Why Bill's having a go at me I don't know. It's all that bitch Tasha's fault, I tried to tell him. He said I should just park somewhere else. He just doesn't get it at all.

He doesn't like it that I won't answer the phone either.

Then he does, he won't tell me who it is.

"I said it's a wrong number but if you can't take my word for it you can bloody well answer it yourself."

It rang and rang until I yanked the socket out the wall.

We sat together on the sofa, but oh so far apart, as we watched a news report of a child who'd been snatched. The parents crying, supporting each other in their grief. I made us a cup of tea then we went to bed, stopping to kiss our sleeping kids but still not speaking.

clash friction mismatch

I get another weird call. I now know Tasha's not making the calls, because I can see her when I answer, but it must be her taking my stuff. Must be.

She wouldn't finish the report I left her. I explained, in front of witnesses and very slowly and carefully so even Tasha couldn't possibly misunderstand how important it was, just before I had to go and see the headmaster at Tom's school. Again.

I'm not paranoid; Tasha really has got it in for me. You'd think even that bitch would have a little compassion for the stress I'm going through. She doesn't need compassion to take my calls; I've diverted my extension to hers.

Bill's sleeping in the spare room. I'm not sleeping at all and the kids are a nightmare. OK, I do see now that I overreacted when Tom wouldn't eat his cereal and I overreacted when the his teacher mentioned it last week. I overreacted when Bill learned his son had the tiniest of bruises and he'd have to collect him from school in future.

I could really do without staying late and finishing a report that Tasha could easily have done. Still, she won't get home any earlier than me – not with that flat tyre.

feud strife antagonism

I wonder how early she arrived today? She got the space, but I got another hour's sleep. I got a family who are talking to me again and a grovelling apology from the school. Seems the teacher really did think I'd hit Tom. She was right to take action if she thought it was true. I suppose I shouldn't have shouted at her for making the suggestion or threatened to hit her. She'll be more careful how she raises such concerns again. I don't suppose Tom will be anymore careful about looking where he's going while he's running around cheeking his mother.

My stuff has still gone and we're no closer to proving who did it. Tasha denies it and I didn't find anything in her desk. If it's not her, who is it? And who is calling?

variance contradiction discord

Victory! The space is free. I can hardly stop myself giggling as I walk to my desk. When I get there, I can't stop screaming. Even over the ringing of the phone I can hear the screaming. The dolls are back, including the one I left in copying. Its hair pulled out in tufts and sharp scratches over its body. The papier-mâche thing is cracked and split. The pictures of the kids…

Vomiting stops the screams.

An arm round my shoulders, a hand offers me tissues. Tasha.

"I saw it, Mandy, My God, I saw it."

Tears in her eyes and she left before me yesterday and wasn't here when I arrived this morning. "Don't look. Come with me." She leads me away.

"Bring her some tea, she's had a horrible shock… Yes, she

saw it," she whispers when a voice asks about my ripped toys, the burn marks on the faces of my kids.

I drink tea and give the police a statement.

quarrel squabble hostility.

I'm taken home. Bill's away at a conference and my boss can't stay. Tasha promises she won't leave me. She understands how I feel you see. She's been through it too. Someone calls her: me. Someone took things from her desk: me. Someone stole her parking space. That was me too, but not my fault.

George gave me a duplicate pass for her car parking space. He said he liked to watch my legs as I got out the car. He used to like watching Tasha's until she asked him not to bring her gifts.

"I thought he'd got the message and left me alone. He got angry though – changed the combination on the front gate without telling me, pestered me with dirty calls, and slashed my car tyre. The police are adding that to the charges against him. At least I know now who was doing these things. It was awful not knowing who to trust."

I cry again and she promises she won't leave; that she's my friend.

Internal, external, eternal.

21. The Restless Sole

Tim looked at the list of potential new names for the chip shop he'd inherited from his dad. He'd sat up until midnight and come up with nothing better than, 'Chipper Chippy', 'Sole Food', 'Tim's Plaice' and 'Diamond Chips'. He threw his pen away in exasperation.

"Careful! I've got enough blue veins without you drawing more."

"Mum! What the hel... "

"Timothy!"

"Sorry, Mum, but you gave me a shock."

"Sorry, dear," she murmured as she studied his list. "Is 'codswallop' another suggestion or an accurate description of the rest?"

"Why are you creeping about?"

"Oh you know I've always been a restless soul and... I'm worried about you."

"I'm fine, honestly," Tim said.

"Fine, but sat up late worrying?"

"All right then... As you can see I'm thinking of renaming this place. 'Cheap as Chips' doesn't suggest the type of quality establishment I want to run, but I'm beginning to see why Dad didn't want to change it."

"He just didn't fancy paying for a new sign."

Tim, not wishing to be disloyal to his dad, said nothing.

"Cheap as chips wasn't so much a business name as a personal motto. He watered the vinegar, did you know that?"

"Mum, this isn't like you."

"It's not how I was before the funeral, but it seems that now's the time to tell the truth. Hmmm, 'Chip off the block'? No, that won't do. He wasn't your real father."

"What!"

"Sorry, dear. Maybe I should have said before?"

"Well, I… Did he know?"

"You were born five months after we got together, weighing eleven pounds. Four stitches I had."

"Mum!"

"Too much information?"

"A bit, yes."

"You won't want to know about your real dad then."

"I'm not sure."

"Me neither. I do know he had a motorbike. They all did."

"But …"

"Sorry, dear. Restless soul like I said."

At that point, Tim's exhaustion caught up with him and he staggered up to bed. The ringing of his phone woke him the next morning.

"Hello? John here… For the interview, but the door's locked."

Tim staggered downstairs and opened the door to Elvis Presley. "Thank goodness, the whole thing was a dream."

"What whole thing?" Elvis asked.

"Something strange happened last night. Or rather tonight. Obviously I'm still asleep."

"Does that mean I'm not getting an interview? I know it looks a bit weird me being dressed like this, especially with the song and all."

"Song?"

"Kirsty McCall? Bloke down the chip shop swears he's Elvis?"

That's when Tim remembered one of the applicants for the position of assistant frier said he had another interview straight afterwards, so would it be OK if he came in his costume? At the time Tim had admired his honesty, but he was beginning to be less enthusiastic about people telling him more of the truth than he wanted to know. "Right. With you now. Come in."

John admitted he was unlikely to be hired as an Elvis impersonator. "With the right costume I look the part and I can sing all his songs, but I don't sound like him and I don't have the moves."

After interviewing John and the next three candidates, one of whom was a delightful young woman, Tim made himself a cup of tea and picked up his list again. He'd scrawled 'Restless Sole' on the bottom. So he had been in this room, not his bed, when he thought his mum dropped her bombshell. That didn't prove he'd been awake though. Maybe he really had dreamed that. Hopefully tonight's dreams would be more pleasant. They would if they featured the girl he'd just hired. He was looking forward to seeing a lot more of her and not just in an apron behind the counter.

"You know, that's not a bad idea."

Tim dropped his mug. "Mum! Stop doing that."

"Sorry, dear. But, I do think it could work."

"What could?"

"Calling it, 'The Restless Sole' and having staff who look like famous people from the past."

"Promote the place as haunted you mean?"

"No, although I did overhear someone say that if your dad knew what you were spending doing this place up he'd turn in his grave! Anyway, as well as Elvis, that pretty girl would look just like Marilyn Monroe in the right dress and wig …"

"You've been hanging about here all day?"

"Don't worry, I don't intend to stay permanently."

"I didn't mean …"

She waved away his attempt to explain. "My point is, celebrities from the past would add a bit of glamour and it would be quite a novelty. All you really need are the right costumes and have them use a catchphrase or two."

"At the risk of sounding like… Dad, costumes would cost money and I don't have any left."

"Sell my wedding ring."

Tim was sceptical. "The ring Mr 'Cheap As Chips' bought you?"

"Actually it was a family heirloom. I was too harsh last night, dear. He never spent more than he had to, but he was a good man in most ways. He'd asked me out lots of times, but I'd always refused until I found out I was expecting you."

"And he asked again?"

"Yes. I was already showing, but all he said was that in my condition I'd be better off dating a lad with a car rather than a bike. It was his way of saying he knew and still thought he'd be lucky to have me."

"That's really quite sweet."

"He often was. Not something he got from is mother. She

said I was a trollop which considering how many boyfriends I ..."

"Mum!"

"Sorry, dear. Anyway he stood up to her and insisted I be given that ring and I'm sure it wasn't just to save him buying another. He promised me if I was faithful and helped with his business he'd bring you up as his own and leave everything to you. We both stuck to that and I don't regret it."

Over the next few nights, Tim and his mum discussed plans for the chip shop and the costumes which would suit his various employees. John was delighted to be employed as Elvis, especially when Tim suggested he sing to entertain waiting customers. He often worked alongside Marilyn Monroe and Winston Churchill. The other shift consisted of Florence Nightingale, Lawrence of Arabia and Amelia Earhart. Cleopatra, Mother Theresa and Freddie Mercury helped out at the weekends or whenever anyone needed a day off. Tim himself dressed as Henry the Eighth.

The chip shop thrived. Tim was so busy working, giving interviews to the papers and local TV channels and taking 'Marilyn' out on Mondays, when they were closed, that it took him a while to realise Mum had settled at last.

Once he did, he missed their chats. He bought a bunch of flowers and took them over to her. He told her how the business was doing and about his relationship. "I'm glad I only pawned your ring, Mum, because I think maybe I'll be needing it myself."

Tim knelt and placed the flowers in front of her headstone. He glanced at the adjacent one, erected in memory of the man who'd brought him up, and winked. "Don't worry, Dad; they were on special offer."

22. The Pier

Carol hesitated outside the bakery, trying to decide between cream-filled chocolate eclairs and jam doughnuts. Which would be most appropriate?

When she and Doug had first visited Southsea as teenagers they used to watch tiny ring doughnuts being made in a special machine at the funfair. They could follow the progress of their treat from raw dough squirted into the bubbling hot fat to sizzling circles dredged in cinnamon sugar and shot into a paper bag. The smell of them cooking and scent of spice had them drooling long before they took possession of the doughnuts. Although they knew they'd be far too hot, they couldn't resist a scalding bite straight away.

She and Doug had returned to Southsea as adults. By then, instead of a day trip by coach, they could afford a week in The King's Hotel. If they bought a snack it was likely to be a cream cake and pot of tea in a café. They visited HMS Victory, Mary Rose, the many fascinating museums, took the hovercraft to the Isle of Wight, strolled around beautiful gardens and lazed on the beach. The last time they'd gone to see Victory, Doug had been in a wheelchair. He could no longer manage the steps around the six decks and had instead watched a film in the gun room. The hotel had provided a specially adapted room and made them just as welcome as always, but Doug hadn't wanted to go back again.

"Carol love, it's no fun for either of us being reminded of

what I can't do now. Let's go somewhere different and try doing new things."

They'd done that for a while. They'd taken a few cruises to exotic places. Doug said the best bit of foreign travel was seeing a new country for the first time and he could easily sit on deck to do that. "And not just a flash of a city as the plane touches down, but a proper look at the coastline as we sail into port."

He'd always been positive, making the most of a situation and trying not to let his condition affect their lives too much.

"Think of the time we'll save not having to drive round in circles looking for an empty space," he'd said when he got his blue badge.

"Great excuse to redecorate," when they'd need to modify the house to accommodate his chair.

He'd encouraged Carol to continue with her career and social life. "I'm fine at home. You know how much I like having a bit of peace to read." He'd even agreed to have a panic button hung round his neck so he could summon help when he needed too.

Then six months ago the tumours spread, the pain increased and doctor had told them there was no longer any hope of recovery or even remission. The doctor arranged a place for him in a hospice. He hadn't taken it yet, but his care needs were increasing. He could barely drag himself out his chair and into bed.

"I just want it to be over, love," he said when she saw him researching suicide methods on the internet.

She'd not been able to reply, not without crying or shouting. They had very little time left, she wouldn't spoil it by losing her temper or hurting him with her own pain.

"I can't do it, Doug. I can't help you kill yourself," she said when he told her of his plans. She pointed out it wasn't legal and how they'd obeyed the rules all their lives. Not that she really cared about that. She'd break any and all laws to get back Doug's health.

"I don't have a life left, Carol."

Carol did, and she couldn't live hers burdened with the guilt of killing her husband. Of wondering how much longer he would have lived, of wishing she'd done more to make his illness tolerable.

They didn't talk about it much. Only once did Carol tell him how desperately she'd miss him, how terrified she was of watching his death. Trouble was, she was already watching it. Doug had become little more than a list of symptoms. The drugs seemed to dull his personality far more effectively than they masked the pain.

Carol had been surprised and pleased when he suggested they revisit Southsea. "That's if it won't be too awful having to push me around and look after me."

"Not at all. We could go out onto the pier and eat doughnuts, like we did when we were kids."

"Perfect."

The doughnut machine had gone and the sun refused to shine, but they both pretended it didn't matter. Just as Carol pretended she thought there was hope of Doug recovering and Doug pretended that death wasn't the only thing he wanted.

"Do you think the starlings still fly in great clouds like they used to?" he asked on their last evening.

They'd gone down to watch the swirling murmurations. It was magical as always. How the birds signalled their wishes and intentions to each other, Carol couldn't fathom, but it was clear that they must and therefore do what was right for the entire group.

"What about those doughnuts then?" Doug had whispered when the birds began to dive under the pier and into their night time shelter.

So Carol left him on the pier while she walked to the bakery and stared in through the window. She still hadn't decided whether to get doughnuts or éclairs when the assistant stuck her head out and said, "If you want anything you need to be quick. We're just about to close."

Carol checked her watch. It was almost five. She'd left Doug in the deepening gloom for nearly an hour. Quickly she bought both éclairs and doughnuts.

She felt guilty about leaving him alone, but understood he'd wanted time to himself. He had little appetite these days so his suggestion she go to buy cakes wasn't because he wanted something to eat. It didn't seem likely he needed the time to think. He often told her thinking was about all he could do and she knew those thoughts were often dark. Doug was in pain, alone on the cold pier on the last day of what would be the last holiday he'd ever take.

As she strode down the wooden boards she called out to Doug. There was no reply and for a moment she wondered if he'd found the strength to wheel himself somewhere warm. Then she saw his chair – empty.

Dropping the cakes, she ran. On the cold seat was an envelope, marked in Doug's untidy writing with her name. She ripped it open and read.

I'm sorry, my love. I know you couldn't watch me die. It's over now and so you don't have to. Remember me as I was when we watched our doughnuts being made and know I'll be waiting on the end of the pier until we're together again. Your Doug. x

As she stared through her tears into the gloom, one last starling flew past, dropping down to join the others. Now, just like Doug, they were all gone from view. Yet she knew they hadn't entirely vanished, but were close by, safe and warm, waiting for the morning light.

23. White Lies And Red Pens

<u>Hayley's first confession.</u>

I know it's daft for a woman in her late twenties to believe in a lucky pen, but I practically fell to pieces when I lost it and almost reverted to being the acne-covered kid who was an object of ridicule for every mean girl in school.

Although I'd never been exactly outgoing, I'd been getting on OK until I turned fifteen. Another quiet girl was a friend. Mostly we kept out of everyone else's way and told ourselves we were better than those who teased us whenever we ventured out of the library.

Then my friend's family moved away. Loneliness would be the worst of it I'd thought, but I was wrong. Some of the mean girls pretended to feel sorry for me and let me join their group. In an effort to fit in I let them talk me into shoplifting. When an older boy asked me out they persuaded me to accept even though I was sure my parents wouldn't be happy.

"Don't worry, say you're with me," one of them said.

The week before our mock exams, I learned my new friends were nothing of the sort, found out the boy had only asked me as a dare, my parents discovered I'd lied to them, and I got caught shoplifting. Naturally my grades were rubbish and I felt my life was pretty much over.

I was a wreck when I came to school. Mrs Bradshaw, my form tutor, calmed me down, persuaded me to tell her everything and then gave me a talking to.

"You've made a few silly mistakes, but you're a bright kid. You've learned your lesson and will pass your exams if you work hard. Your spots aren't worse than those of half the school and they'll be gone soon. You're a nice person and will make real friends."

She gave me a pen to remind me of all that. A proper cartridge one in a lovely deep red colour.

I took it straight into the next class and saw someone had damaged one of the desks, meaning I wouldn't get to sit on my own. The first few to come in sniggered and sat elsewhere. Then David James arrived. Short, shy and clumsy David had little in common with the England goalkeeper of the same name. He bumped into the desk and asked if he could sit by me. Not exactly an honour as he was only slightly less unpopular than me, but I think he was trying to be kind.

After that we always sat together for maths and physics. We weren't boy and girlfriend or anything, but we talked a bit and worked together on projects. If I saw him around he'd nod or raise a hand to acknowledge me.

The same week as Mrs Bradshaw gave me the pen, I got a letter from my old friend suggesting we be pen pals. Things were looking up.

By the time I'd passed my exams, all written in my lucky pen, my spots were clearing. I got a decent job, made friends and went on dates. The pen came with me everywhere. I used it to sign job applications and apply for a driving licence. Using the pen, or reaching into a pocket and feeling the familiar smooth surface, or even just knowing it was in my bag, helped me through all sorts of situations.

Yeah, that's all a bit daft, but not as daft as the fact that I managed to lose it.

<u>Rob's first confession.</u>

When my sister told me she'd lost her lucky pen I was surprised. I hadn't realised she still believed in all that nonsense.

"The pen isn't lucky, Hayley. It was that teacher's pep talk which sorted you out."

"That probably helped, but the pen does too. Or did."

She told me she'd split up with her boyfriend. As I'd never taken to him that seemed like good news to me, but I wasn't sure how the pen came into it. "He dumped you because you didn't have a pen on you?"

"No, of course not. Actually I split up with him because we kept rowing over stupid things and I could see we didn't have anything in common, but I was still sad about it. I bought myself a huge bar of chocolate, and a magazine. I settled down with those and a mug of tea, ready to cheer myself up with the puzzles when I discovered the pen was gone. The last time I know I had it we'd been getting on fine."

I wasn't convinced there was any connection and said so.

"I haven't had any good luck since," Hayley claimed.

"But it's not even the same pen!"

"Of course it is."

I took a deep breath. "Remember how you couldn't find it the day you started study leave and thought someone had stolen it?"

"And you found it down the back of the sofa. That was one of the things which convinced me to stop looking at life in such a negative way and trust the pen to help me out."

"I didn't find it down the sofa. I got you a replacement."

"Oh. But …"

"See, it's not the pen which helped, but the belief it gave you in yourself."

"I don't know what to say."

"That it was lovely of me to do that and, now you know, you'll do me something nice in return. Bake me a lemon drizzle cake perhaps?"

"Yes, all right but first help me get a replacement for the replacement pen. If I can get one just like the other two, I'm sure it'll work just as well."

"I'm sure you're right. Why not try Rodger's Stationery in the High Street? That's where I got it. They might have old stock or know where you could try."

<u>Hayley's second confession.</u>

At first I wasn't sure it really was David James in the stationery shop, but then he dropped the box of cards he'd been refilling the shelves with. His clumsiness might not have improved but let me tell you, the rest of him had.

"Hayley! Nice to see you," he said.

Perhaps Mrs Bradshaw was right in saying I didn't look so dreadful at fifteen because, although I thought I'd improved since, David clearly had no trouble recognising me. I helped him pick up the scattered cards and we chatted for a bit about old times before I explained about the pen. I blushed as I told him he was one of the good things which resulted from it. I admit I knew he'd be flattered if I said it, that I'd blush as I did and that I look pretty when I blush.

"It was a good thing for me too," he said. He blushed as well.

He was so sweet about it all. Unlike my brother, he didn't make fun of my belief the pen had helped, nor my desire to get another one. After I'd described it in detail and we'd examined the stock and found nothing the same he offered to try to track one down.

"I'll ask around. It might take some time though. Shall I take your number and give you a call if I find anything out?"

I scribbled it down and handed it to the man who'd once been a boy who was kind to me when I really needed a friend. It seemed that just searching for a new pen had brought the return of my good luck.

<u>David's first confession.</u>

Seeing Hayley Morgan again and then having her say nice things to me was rather a shock. That's my excuse for misleading her a bit and I'm sticking to it. I knew exactly where I could get a pen like the one she'd described, but I pretended not to be sure just so she'd stay and talk to me for a while. I'd always liked her at school, but I was just as shy and self conscious as I'm now realising she was and so never tried to be more than slightly friendly.

Now I've got her number, I'm not sure what to do. Planning how to get a pretty girl to go out with me isn't one of my strong points. I vaguely thought I'd keep ringing her with updates and make out it was really difficult to get hold of a pen like the one she wanted. Then when I eventually 'found' one I'd suggest meeting for a drink in the evening instead of her taking time off work to come to the shop. Maybe she'd see my handing it to her as some kind of good omen and want to keep me around.

Trouble is, I knew it wasn't on for me to outright lie to her, not when it was all thought out in advance like that, rather than a spur of the moment omission. What to do?

<u>Hayley's third confession.</u>

I was fully aware David had said he'd call me if he managed to track down my pen and I didn't doubt his word, but I let that sort of slip my mind and went in to ask him if he'd heard anything.

The reduced price diaries, which had been in a neat stack, tumbled across the counter. "Actually... I should have one by the weekend."

"That's brilliant! I don't suppose... um, well could I buy you dinner or something to thank you for all your trouble?"

"It wasn't any trouble, really."

"Oh." That was disappointing. I'd rather counted on being allowed to show my gratitude.

"Perhaps I could take you out, well just because ..." he said.

Yes! "I'd like that. Thank you."

<u>Rob's second confession.</u>

I was dead chuffed when David asked me to be his best man. I'm not his best friend of course, but the chap who has that honour is as shy as him and suggested David pick someone who could take charge and make a speech. No problem there. I reckon I was born with most of my sister's share of confidence.

She's got some now though. Love can do that for a person. She and David make a great couple. I've only got one concern about their relationship. Hayley is going to have to promise me that when they have a baby she only lets her husband hold my niece or nephew when he's sitting down. Don't want the poor kid dropped on its head.

I'm totally taking the credit for getting them together. She'd never have gone into the stationery shop where he worked if I hadn't made up that line about her lucky pen being a fake. Don't get me wrong, I don't believe the pen her teacher gave her had any special powers, but I really did find the original down the back of the sofa. I only said I hadn't so she would realise she wasn't heading for disaster just because she'd lost it for real.

Now, how do I word this in the speech so I look like a good guy rather than a total liar?

<u>David's second confession.</u>

I'm really nervous about making my speech at the wedding.

Rob said not to worry. "I'll yack on until everyone has had enough and then all you need do is say 'thanks for coming' and propose another toast and everyone will be delighted."

It's not a bad plan and I think I can do my small part. Yes, of course I can. I'll have Hayley, who'll be my wife by then, at my side. And I know she'll have my lucky red pen with her. She still carries it everywhere.

Yes, it's my lucky pen. You see, the reason I knew where to get hold of one just like that which Hayley had described was that Mrs Bradshaw had given me one. I'd not had it long when I saw Hayley sitting alone in maths and got up the nerve to sit with her. Shall I tell her now, or wait until the honeymoon?

<u>Mrs Bradshaw has the last word.</u>

Well look at that, another wedding invitation! Who is it this time? Ah, Hayley Morgan and David James. I always knew those two would get together, although I confess I hadn't expected it to take quite so long as this.

24. In Charlotte's Book

"You OK?" Charlotte asked when she'd made the coffee.

"Not really," Isobel admitted.

"Empty nest syndrome? I thought that might be an issue." She waved her hand in a 'give me a moment' gesture and left the kitchen. She returned with a huge, tatty looking book. "Here read this. It changed my life."

Isobel flicked through the closely packed pages. "It'll take me forever to read that."

"Then it'll change your life forever, won't it?"

Isobel rolled her eyes. "Anyway, empty nest isn't my problem. Quite the opposite. I was looking forward to getting my life back once the brats were off my hands. Not that I don't love them, but I thought with them living away, things would get easier and I'd have some time to be myself."

"But it's not worked out like that?"

"No. It has for Chris. He's reduced his golf handicap, but …" Isobel shrugged. She'd already discussed the unfairness of this with her work colleague Babs.

"He plays golf alone?"

Was Charlotte hinting the same thing Babs had suggested? "I'm positive he really is playing golf. Sorry, you're the last person I should be moaning to."

Charlotte's rotten husband had cheated on her. In Isobel's

opinion that was probably the best thing he did as it forced Charlotte to face facts and divorce him; a great relief to her friends and family. The man had been a bully. He put her down all the time, sapped her confidence.

Charlotte placed her hand on Isobel's shoulder. "Hey, I'm your friend and you were there for me. I'm exactly who you should be talking to. Moan away, it might help. With Steve I never did, just pretended it was all fine. Things might have been better if I'd spoken out."

"I suppose you're right." Isobel and Charlotte's other friends would have realised how bad things had got. They could have pointed out Steve's behaviour wasn't normal, or reasonable. It was hard to do that when Charlotte pretended to be happy.

Isobel indulged in a moan about how Chris took her for granted. "On the weekends we have a lie-in and big breakfast. Then he goes off to golf and comes home to a tidy house, cupboards full of food and dinner in the oven. It's not fair."

Without Babs egging her on and saying he shouldn't treat her like a servant, Isobel soon trailed off. "He doesn't really do anything wrong, it's just that he seems to think that stuff all happens by magic."

"I know I'm not one to talk, but maybe you should tell him?"

Isobel grinned at her friend. Charlotte had learned her lesson; she now had a lovely new man who treated her well, and wasn't afraid to express herself.

"I have said I'm fed up and to be fair I think he'd worked that out himself. Sometimes he mentions I've not seen you for a while or that I should get a hobby. Probably, like you, he thinks I'm missing the kids, but I don't really have time."

"Hmmm. Try to make time to read the book. Please."

Isobel took it with her when she left her friend's home. As she carried it out to her car she remembered listening to the radio at her grandmother's house. There used to be a children's programme which began by asking if the listeners were sitting comfortably, as they were about to be told a story. Isobel wasn't particularly comfortable. She'd intended to go straight into town after the visit but decided to go home and change first. She'd got dressed up for the first time in ages to meet Charlotte and had forgotten that pair of shoes squashed her toes and rubbed under her ankle bone. She wasn't going to suffer in them all round the supermarket.

Once home, Isobel decided she might as well put the kettle on. She'd had coffee with Charlotte but that didn't quench her thirst like a cup of tea. Isobel opened the book, intending to read a few pages as she waited for the water to boil, so she could tell Charlotte she'd given it a try.

The scruffy exterior of the book hadn't prepared her for what lay inside. The words were lovely, almost magical. There was a rhythm to them which made reading the tiny print as easy as listening to joyful music. As the main character wandered through woods and out into open fields, Charlotte felt as though she were walking by her side. She could almost feel sunlight on her face and soft grass under her feet. She was as eager as the girl in the story was to see what lay on the other side of the hedge.

Isobel was surprised to realise she'd finished her tea; she couldn't remember making it. Reluctantly she tore herself away from the book to go shopping. As she filled the supermarket trolley it occurred to her she was hardly ever out in the fresh air. Stuffy train to work, stuffy office, stuffy train home where she cleaned and cooked before slumping exhausted in front of the TV; those were her habitats. She did pass through fields and woodland, but it was just a blur in the background as she thought about the next item on her 'to do' list.

Chris was already home when she got back with the shopping. He actually came out to the car and helped her carry in the bags.

"Everything OK?" he asked.

"I'm just a bit late as I popped into Charlotte's for coffee and we got talking."

As she started to put away the food, Isobel saw she'd rushed out leaving her mug on the table and a used teabag in the sink. They hadn't been magically cleared away.

"Oh good. How is she?" Chris asked.

"Make us a cup of tea while I finish sorting this lot out and I'll tell you."

Chris rinsed out her mug to reuse and put all three teabags in the bin when he'd made the drinks. Perhaps he wasn't so bad as she'd claimed when she moaned to Charlotte.

"I'm guessing dinner isn't ready," Chris said.

Or maybe he really was. Unless Charlotte was right that she just needed to remind him these tasks had to be done by someone. Before she could explain that she'd bleached all the grouting in the bathroom and polished the glass in all their photo frames before going out, he suggested they get a takeaway.

As usual he told her about his game over their evening meal. His talk of the green and woods reminded her of the words in the book and unusually she listened to him. As he described searching through undergrowth for a lost ball and hitting another into the lake, Isobel remembered a joke about golf spoiling a nice walk. She'd like a walk even if it involved golf.

"Are you playing tomorrow?" she asked.

"I was thinking of it, unless you'd rather I stayed in?"

"Actually I thought I might come and caddy for you."

"That'd be great." He looked delighted.

"It'll cost you though."

"Oh?"

She indicated their dirty plates. "You sort those out."

"Deal."

Isobel decided to read a little more of Charlotte's book before the TV programme she usually watched came on. The girl in the story found a stile in the hedge and climbed up on it. From the higher position she looked down on a village and recognised it as the home she'd been searching for. As she described the people who lived there, Isobel found herself drawn into their lives. She was torn between reading on quickly to learn all she could about them and studying every sentence for the clues the girl dropped about her exile from those she knew and loved.

So engrossed was she that nothing outside the book existed for her until Chris gently nudged her.

"It's getting cold," he said.

Isobel glanced from the mug of hot chocolate he'd made, to the clock. It was already past the time she usually went to bed!

Golf was quite fun really. She'd never considered playing as she had no skill at that sort of thing, but it was a nice walk, she chatted to the other players and caddy and Chris didn't seem bothered that she couldn't tell one club from another. When they got home Chris didn't tell her about the game as she'd seen it all, so talked of other things. Nothing amazing, but it made a pleasant change.

Isobel read Charlotte's book on the train to work. In it the girl talked about her travels, giving tempting details of interesting sounding food. Isobel decided to try cooking some of it. She might as well; she'd been so busy reading each day she'd neglected to make her usual meal plans and shopping lists. She and Chris visited small speciality shops, searching for the required ingredients and they cooked the dishes together. Somehow there was time for that. She'd not really been as busy as she'd thought; just stuck in a rut of cooking the same things, watching the same things on TV and just possibly inventing a few extra tasks to fill the gap left by her departed children.

Charlotte had told her to make time to read the book and she did just that. Instead of listening to Babs' constant criticism of everyone and everything, she read a few pages in her lunch break. Somehow the cheeriness of the character's words helped Isobel avoid the usual mid-afternoon mood slump. Reading again on the return journey meant she arrived home with a smile on her face. She discovered that if she didn't rush around vacuuming, putting clothes in the wash and dusting everything in sight the moment she'd got in from work, that Chris would tackle some of the most urgent tasks. She began to feel less drained and less put upon.

The girl in the book had felt the need to alter her appearance and had a dramatically different hairstyle. As the story was set in the past, the look wouldn't now be considered very radical. Actually it might suit Isobel and, as her inspiration had discovered, it would be easy to care for. Instead of golf both days the next week, she visited the salon on Saturday. Her new look generated lots of compliments, especially from Chris. Isobel instantly felt younger and more confident. That and the exercise from golf, plus her more varied diet seemed to give her more energy.

When she got home there was a message from Charlotte to say she was getting married! Isobel was pleased at her friend's good news but even more so at the happiness and optimism in her voice. It was such a welcome change in her friend.

Could the book really have made the difference? Charlotte was sure it had and perhaps it was helping Isobel too? It didn't look much, not even a dust jacket with a picture on. Just the title and author name in almost worn away gold lettering on a dull green background.

As Isobel had predicted, it was taking her a long time to read. She'd barely begun the second chapter. How fantastic might her life be by the end?

The character in the book revealed that one reason for her leaving home was the ending of an unhappy relationship. During her travels she'd met someone new. A man who cared for and respected her. That sounded a lot like Charlotte's experience.

Isobel rang her friend. "Congratulations! It's wonderful news."

"Isn't it? I can hardly believe it but I just know it's true and this time I'm doing the right thing." She chattered on, bubbling with excitement about the wedding plans and the happy life she'd lead with her new husband.

"Ooops! Totally forgot to ask you to be my matron of honour. You will won't you?"

"Of course."

"And wear a fabulous dress. I've chosen it already. Hang on I'll email the picture."

As Isobel listened to more details than she really needed of the planned honeymoon she started up her computer and opened the link. The dress was hideous.

"Ha, ha, got you!" Charlotte squealed.

Isobel giggled. Not so much because of the joke, but because her friend was back. The crazy enthusiasm and silly sense of fun was exactly how Charlotte had been when they were teenagers.

Isobel hadn't been so exuberant. She'd been the calming influence. The practical one who reminded her friend to do her homework or that if they didn't leave right now they'd miss the last bus back home. She'd been just as happy though in her own, quieter, way. Just like she was now.

After she'd finished talking to Charlotte, Isobel made herself a cup of tea and sat down with the book. She didn't open it. She wasn't sure she wanted to read on. Charlotte had been so sure it had changed her life and Isobel was almost certain it had done the same for her. Isobel didn't need Charlotte's kind of happiness. She had simply wanted her life back and not to be taken for granted and that's just what she had.

She called Charlotte back. "That book, how does it end?"

"I thought you were reading it?"

"I was honestly, but …"

"OK, I confess I didn't get past chapter three. It really is a good story, but somehow I didn't want to continue."

"I've almost finished chapter two. I think I should stick there."

"I can't say why, but I agree. Perhaps you can pass it on to someone else who might enjoy it?"

"Good idea."

She'd give it to Babs at work. That woman would need six chapters at least.

Thank you for reading this book. I hope you enjoyed it. If you did, I'd really appreciate it if you could leave a short review on Amazon and/or Goodreads.

To learn more about my writing life, hear about new releases and get a free exclusive ebook, sign up to my newsletter – subscribepage.io/ItLSNa or you can find the link on my website patsycollins.co.uk

<u>More books by Patsy Collins</u>

Novels

Firestarter
Escape To The Country
A Year And A Day
Paint Me A Picture
Leave Nothing But Footprints
Acting Like A Killer

Little Mallow cosy mystery series

Disguised Murder and Community Spirit in Little Mallow
Dependable Friends and Deceitful Neighbours
in Little Mallow
Deadly Words and Innocent Gossip in Little Mallow

Non-fiction

From Story Idea To Reader
(co-written with Rosemary J. Kind)

A Year Of Ideas:
365 sets of writing prompts and exercises

Short story collections

Over The Garden Fence
Up The Garden Path
Through The Garden Gate
In The Garden Air
Beyond The Garden Wall

No Family Secrets
Can't Choose Your Family
Keep It In The Family
Family Feeling
Happy Families

All That Love Stuff
With Love And Kisses
Lots Of Love
Love Is The Answer

Slightly Spooky Stories I
Slightly Spooky Stories III
Slightly Spooky Stories IV
Slightly Spooky Stories V

Just A Job
Perfect Timing
A Way With Words
Dressed To Impress
Coffee & Cake
Not A Drop To Drink
Criminal Intent
Crime In Mind
Making A Move
Days To Remember
A Clean Bill Of Health
Your Good Health